THE IMPOSSIBLE QUEST

FOR MY THREE CHILDREN,
BEN, TIM AND ELLA

First American Edition 2016
Kane Miller, A Division of EDC Publishing

Text copyright © Kate Forsyth 2015

First published by Scholastic Press, a division of Scholastic Australia Pty Limited in 2015.
Cover illustration, gifts, and maps on page iv and viii by Jeremy Reston.
Map on page vi by Radhiah Chowdhury, copyright © Scholastic Australia, 2015.
Logo design by blacksheep-uk.com.
This edition published under license from Scholastic Australia Pty Limited.
Internal photography: brick texture on page i © GiorgioMagini|istockphoto.com;
castle on page ii and folios © ivan-96|istockphoto.com; map compass and texture on page vi ©
Dmytro Denysov|Dreamstime.com; reverse skull on page 150 © Frankie_Lee|istockphoto.com.

For information contact:
Kane Miller, A Division of EDC Publishing
P.O. Box 470663
Tulsa, OK 74147-0663
www.kanemiller.com
www.edcpub.com
www.usbornebooksandmore.com

Library of Congress Control Number: 2015938802

Printed and bound in the United States of America

2 3 4 5 6 7 8 9 10

ISBN: 978-1-61067-416-4

KATE FORSYTH

THE IMPOSSIBLE QUEST

3

THE BEAST OF BLACKMOOR BOG

Kane Miller
A DIVISION OF EDC PUBLISHING

Map of Wolfhaven & Surrounding Lands

The Witchwood

Crowthorne Castle

Blackmoor Bog

Rosemorran River

to
Crowthorne Castle

Castle
Ruins

Rosemorran River

N
E
W
S

Blackmoor
Bog

The
Rowan Tree

to
Ashbyrne

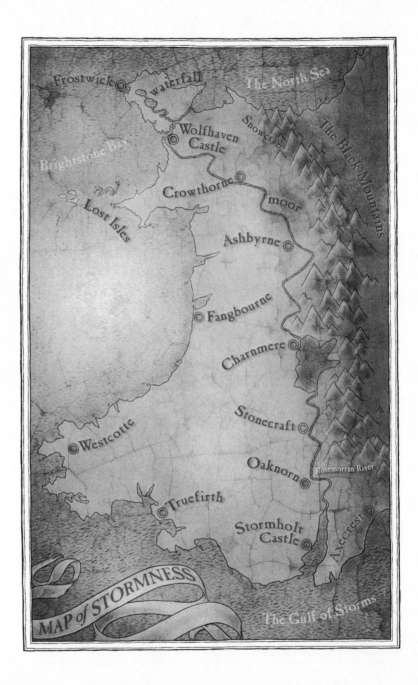

THE
THIEF

"Stop, thief!"

Sebastian spun on his heel, one hand flying to his belt where his sword used to hang. Nobody was pointing at him, though. He tried to relax, his blood hammering with the sudden rush of nervous energy.

He was finding it hard being back in a town, jostled and jolted on all sides by strangers, not knowing who was a friend or an enemy. It had been three days since he and his friends had fled the Witchwood, but Sebastian was certain that Lord and Lady Mortlake were still hunting them down. The Mortlakes had proven to be utterly ruthless and had powerful magic at their command. Sebastian hoped he was not walking into a trap.

"Stop that thief!" someone shouted again.

Behind him, Elanor cried out as she was elbowed to the side by a burly butcher in a stained apron. "Sorry, missy," he said. "Got to join the hue and cry."

Shopkeepers ran out from their stalls, snatching up cudgels. No one liked a thief.

"Stop him!" the cries rose up.

"He went that way!"

"No, that way! Cut him off!"

Sebastian put his arm out to steady Elanor, who was in danger of being crushed. "I wonder what he stole?" he asked.

Elanor didn't answer. She was looking first one way, then another. Alleyways stretched in all directions, as far as the eye could see. They all looked much the same: cramped, dirty, crowded and hung with clotheslines. People pushed and shoved, shouting out their wares, arguing over prices, elbowing their way past. A skinny dog was nosing through some rubbish in a corner, while hens pecked hopefully at the dirt.

An enormous pink and black pig oinked from where it lay in its muddy pen.

"We shouldn't have tried to cut through the market, Sebastian, I knew it was a mistake," Elanor said.

"I thought it'd be a shortcut," he explained, stepping back against the wall to allow a heavily-laden donkey to push past.

"If we could just get higher, we could see which way the castle is." Elanor looked up at the stained and patched walls towering high on either side. The buildings seemed to lean together overhead, which made it impossible to see out.

"Look, there are some stairs. Perhaps they'll lead us back to the road." Sebastian led the way along the hot, stinking lane, bumped on all sides by bustling women with baskets, burly men shouldering barrels, smiling shopkeepers thrusting rolls of wool and silk under his nose and a water seller carrying two sloshing buckets on a yoke.

They reached the steps and began to climb up to a landing. From there, Sebastian could see the gray hulk of Crowthorne Castle squatting far above them.

The narrow arrow slits made the castle seem angry and unapproachable.

Sebastian felt a pang of anxiety. Perhaps the others had been right and it was a mistake to come to Crowthorne Castle. Sebastian hardened his jaw. No. He was right. Four people could not fight against a whole army alone. They needed help.

It had been almost two weeks since Wolfhaven Castle, Lady Elanor's home, had been attacked by an army led by Lord Mortlake, who ruled the neighboring land of Frostwick. It seemed the Lord of Frostwick coveted the Lord of Wolfhaven's fertile fields and orchards, and the ease of trade given by his river and sea harbor. Among his army were the sinister bog-men, creatures of some foul dark magic that were nearly impossible to kill.

Sebastian had been on the run ever since, along with Lady Elanor, the daughter of the Lord of Wolfhaven, Tom, the cook's son, and Quinn, apprentice to the Grand Teller of Wolfhaven. They were all determined to rescue the enslaved people of Wolfhaven, but argued constantly over the best way to do it.

For Sebastian, it was frustrating. He was the son of a lord; his father was the ruler of Ashbyrne, a country to the south. He had been trained from birth to be a knight. All the others—and especially that pot boy Tom—should acknowledge his greater expertise. When Sebastian said they should go to the Lady of Crowthorne Castle and ask for her help, the others should have just agreed and done it.

But no! Quinn thought they should stay focused on their search for the four magical beasts, as Arwen, the Grand Teller, had told them to do. She wanted them to head south into the moors when they had no supplies, no directions, and Sebastian's boot sole was flapping like a gossip's tongue.

Meanwhile, Elanor worried that Lady Ravenna of Crowthorne might be in league with the Lord of Frostwick. But everyone knew the lady was already rich, with peat mines and coal works—she had no reason to invade Wolfhaven.

Then Tom had reminded Sebastian of the last time they had gone to seek help at his insistence. Sebastian's ears had burned. But if they had not gone knocking on the door of Frostwick Castle, they would never have found out it was Lord Mortlake behind the attack, and they would never have been able to rescue the unicorn he had kept captive in his stables.

The unicorn was one of the four beasts Sebastian and his friends were searching for, and it had given them all hope that perhaps their quest was not so impossible after all. Without Quickthorn's sharp horn and swift hooves, they would never have been able to fight off the bog-men on their trail and would never have found the griffin hidden in the Witchwood. Tom would never have been able to tame the great winged beast with his magical flute and would never have soared through the sky on Rex's back while Sebastian had to trudge along on his own aching feet. Tom should be grateful that Sebastian had made them go to Frostwick Castle!

So Sebastian had announced that he would go to Crowthorne Castle by himself, which only caused another round of arguments. In the end, Quinn and Tom made camp and stayed behind on the moors to guard the animals (which now included a wolf cub,

Wulfric, as well as Tom's old wolfhound, Fergus), while Sebastian and Elanor had gone off together.

"Don't you worry, Sebastian, if you get locked up in a tower, me and Rex will come and save you," Tom had said, stroking the feathered neck of the griffin.

That pot boy could be so annoying.

"Look!" Elanor cried, pointing. "There's the thief."

From the stairs, Sebastian and Elanor could look straight down on the market square that dominated the center of town. The thief was bolting down the square, leaving chaos and destruction behind him.

He kicked over a barrel of ale and sent it splashing across the cobblestones so the people chasing him slipped and fell. He leapt over a fruit stand, then seized the apples and used them to pelt his pursuers. He swung off a string of onions and knocked the burly butcher off his feet. He seized an armful of clay pots and hurled them behind him. He ducked this way, then that, so two stall holders chasing him ran headlong into each other and were knocked off their feet. He slid right through the legs of a plump washer-woman, then ran up the broad back of a pie man, somersaulting over his head.

The thief came closer and closer to the edge of the square. Hands reached out to grab him from all sides, but he ducked and weaved and leapt and dived so nimbly no one could keep hold of him.

"He's as slippery as a greased pig," Sebastian said admiringly, thinking how useful the thief would be on a mob-ball team.

Elanor leaned forward, her gaze intent. "Sebastian, don't you think that thief looks familiar?"

"Like who?"

"Jack Spry, the boy who jumped out of a pie at the midsummer feast."

Sebastian squinted at the thief, who was now running along the top of a row of stalls, sending pots crashing. He had a mop of matted black curls and laughing black eyes, and he seemed to be taking pleasure in causing as much havoc as possible. "Maybe."

Soldiers in black-and-white livery ran into the square. The shape of a crow was emblazoned on their jerkins. The crowd pressed back against the wall, making room for them as they charged up the square, pikes held high. The thief waited, laughing, till they were almost upon him, then somersaulted right over their heads.

A goose girl was herding her flock into the square below Elanor and Sebastian. The thief bolted through the flock, causing the geese to rear back and hiss in alarm. The goose girl did her best to keep her flock together with a willow switch, but the thief waved his arms and shouted, so the geese took to the air, honking loudly. The soldiers shouted in alarm and tried to protect their faces as geese flapped their wings and snapped their beaks.

The thief then spun the goose girl around, held her in front of him as a shield and seized her basket of goose eggs. With a strong arm and excellent aim, he began to sling eggs at the soldiers. One smashed on a soldier's head, another on a soldier's chest. One broke right under a soldier's foot, making him slip over. Another smashed on the sharp blade of a halberd, sending a spray of egg everywhere. Soon, every one of the soldiers was stumbling around, being pecked by geese and covered in goo.

Sebastian couldn't help laughing.

The thief took advantage of the chaos to leap up onto a shop awning. He grabbed a drainpipe and swarmed up it, then ran across a rooftop, leaped across the gap and kept on running. Reaching a lane that was too wide to jump, he simply ran over the clothesline as easily as if it was a plank of wood. Over the rooftops he raced, jumping, vaulting, hurdling and veering his way through the chimney pots and dormer windows.

Cursing, wiping egg goo from their eyes, the soldiers ran after him. Some pounded through the alleyways, others clambered up drainpipes and over the roof, their boots thundering on the tiles.

The thief kept on running, astonishingly swift. He caught hold of the end of a clothesline and used it to swing out and over the heads of the soldiers. As they tried to jab him with their pikes, he landed on the sheer face of the cliff, just below where Elanor and Sebastian were watching.

"That *is* Jack Spry," Elanor said, looking worried. "What is he doing here? Last time I saw him, he was escaping Wolfhaven Castle with my family silver."

Sebastian gazed at the boy in surprise. He looked so different dressed in rags, his face grimy, his curls matted with leaves. Jack looked up and saw them, and stopped for a moment, mouth open in shock. Then he grinned, waved his arm and began to climb their way.

The troop leader lifted his bow high, fitting an arrow to the string. Jack scrambled faster. Sebastian was too far away to hear the string twang, but he saw the arrow fly upward, swift and true. Jack scrabbled sideways, but he was tiring, sweat running down through the grime on his face. The arrow hit the rock face only inches from his fingers. The thief flinched back and lost his grip. He managed to claw at the cliff with his hand, but it was clear he wouldn't be able to cling on much longer.

"Help him!" Elanor cried to Sebastian. She tried to reach him, but her arms weren't long enough.

Sebastian flung himself down on the ground and reached down as far as he could. He managed to grab at Jack's arm, catching hold of his skinny wrist just as his fingers slid free of their grip. For a moment, Jack swung free. Sebastian's shoulder screamed with pain. Groaning with the effort, he managed to haul the boy up and over the edge of the landing.

"Run!" Jack panted. "She'll see us dead if she catches us."

"Us?" Sebastian began, but Jack was already bolting up the stairs and Elanor followed, skirts caught up in her hands. Sebastian looked down and saw the soldiers running for the stairs. He ran after the other two. "But why are we running?" he panted to Elanor, as they pounded up the stairs. "We're not the ones they're after."

Elanor shook her head, too short of breath to answer him. Sebastian wanted to point out that now it looked as though they were in league with Jack, but all of his energy was poured into their steady ascent of the stairs.

Up, up, up, they ran, panting. The road was above them. Sebastian lengthened his stride. Through the pounding of the blood in his ears, he could hear a strange creaking sound. It sounded like the turning of a windmill. He concentrated on forcing his tired legs to keep on running. Up, up, up, he ran.

At last, Sebastian scrambled the last few steps, using his hands as if climbing a ladder, and half fell onto the road.

A heavy hand fell on his shoulder and dragged him up.

"A good haul this evening," a man's deep voice said. "Three thieves instead of one. Lady Ravenna will be pleased."

THE
CASTLE DUNGEONS

"We're not thieves!" Sebastian protested.

"Is that so?" the man said. He set Sebastian on his feet so roughly he almost fell. "Yet we caught you fair and square, aiding and abetting a known thief that the Crowthorne Guards have been hunting for days." He jerked a squat thumb at Jack, who was wriggling and squirming in the firm grip of two grinning soldiers.

"He was going to fall!"

"And now he'll be executed instead," one of the soldiers said. "I don't think he'll be thanking you tomorrow."

"And you'll be wishing you fell to your deaths too," another guffawed.

"I tell you, sir, with all honor, my lady and I are not thieves." Sebastian straightened his back and invested his voice with as much authority as he could.

"Then why did you run?"

Sebastian had no ready answer.

"Lord Sebastian speaks true," said Elanor. "We are not thieves. I am Lady Elanor Belleterre of Wolfhaven Castle and my companion is Lord Sebastian Byrne of Ashbyrne Castle. We've come here on a mission of utmost urgency and must be escorted to her ladyship as soon as possible."

The lead trooper was taken aback. He scrutinized them carefully. Elanor's gown, though stained and torn, was clearly silk, the embroidery sewn with gilt thread. Her shoes, worn and muddied, were nonetheless made of golden leather. Sebastian's jerkin was made of red velvet and he carried a shield with a red lion slung over one shoulder.

"If you lot are lords and ladies, what're you doing associating with a lowlife like him?" One of the soldiers shook Jack like a terrier shaking a rat.

Elanor took a deep breath. Sebastian glared at her, willing her to say nothing.

"He's my fool," Elanor said.

They all laughed and laughed.

"You must take *us* for fools," the lead trooper said at last, grinning and wiping a tear from his eye. "Her *fool*!" he laughed. "Take them to the dungeons, lads!"

"But no! Sir!" Both Elanor and Sebastian protested, but no one paid them any mind. As they were marched up the steep road towards the castle, Sebastian began to wonder how the soldiers could possibly have beaten them to the top of the stairs. When he had saved Jack from falling, the soldiers had all been clustered at the foot of the cliff, at least a hundred feet below. How had they gotten up to the road so fast?

At the next curve of the road he had his answer. A giant contraption made of wood and rope stood in a lookout carved by the side of the road. Two oxen were harnessed to a giant wheel, from which hung a wooden platform six feet square. A complex system of ropes and pulleys made it clear the platform could be raised up and down the cliff as the oxen turned the tread wheel. It would be an easy way of lowering people and objects from the castle to the town, and back again. It was the creaking of the wheel that had made that strange windmill sound.

The soldiers pushed the three children past the oxen, waiting patiently in their harness, and around a steep curve in the road. Above them loomed Crowthorne Castle, black and forbidding. Above its battlements, the sky was smeared with red.

One of the soldiers muttered something to the troop leader, who answered, "Blasted if I know, Roy. Her ladyship will have the truth out of them, never fear."

Sebastian was pushed through the castle gate, under a heavy portcullis of sharpened steel stakes. He only took in an impression of dimness and dampness. Ahead was a great square keep. To one side, a guard-house; to the other, what smelled like stables. Jack was still struggling to break free. A blow from his captors seemed to daze him and the soldiers had to half carry, half drag him after that. As they reached the guardhouse, Jack broke free and ran, proving that it had been an act all along. It took five soldiers to seize him again.

Elanor walked quietly, her head high, her tattered skirts shush-shushing against the cobblestones. The soldiers who escorted her held her arms gently, and when one stood aside to let her pass through the doorway into the guardhouse, she thanked them politely.

They were taken into the guardhouse, lit by smoking lanterns on poles. The soldiers each grabbed one. The children were then pushed down a long flight of steps, along a hallway, past rooms where guards sat in their shirts and breeches, glancing up curiously from their games of cards and dice, down more steps, along a corridor, down more steps, along a passageway, down more steps and finally into what felt like a tunnel.

The troop leader grabbed a ring of keys from a hook on the wall and ordered them to march along the narrow passage. It smelled terrible. Iron-barred doors were set along the wall. Prisoners shook the bars, reaching out pleading hands, begging for help, for justice, for release.

"Please, don't give me to the Beast," one shrieked.

"No, not the Beast!" wailed another.

Elanor shot a terrified glance at Sebastian. ". . . the Beast . . . ?" she whispered. He shook his head, not knowing what to say.

At last, the soldiers reached a small square room, with a table and a hard wooden stool. Half of the room was a prison cell, divided from the guardroom by thick iron bars. The troop leader unlocked the gate and the three children were pushed inside the cell.

"We'll leave them here in the holding cell a while, just in case their story is true," he told the soldiers.

"You can't believe that bag of moonshine about them being lords and ladies," one said incredulously.

"And fools," another sniggered. "That's easy enough to believe."

"Not for a moment," the troop leader replied, "but I believe in taking no chances."

The soldiers marched away, taking the lantern with them. Sebastian, Elanor and Jack were left alone in the prison cell, in utter, deafening darkness.

CHATTING ABOUT OLD TIMES

Slowly a magical, silvery light rose and filled the cell.

Elanor was breathing on her moonstone ring, the Traveler's Stone, conjuring light from its mysterious depths.

Jack Spry stared at her, then at the ring, then back at Elanor. He took a deep breath and shrugged one shoulder. "You're the fool," he said to Elanor. "You almost had them."

"I was trying to help you," Elanor replied.

"I don't need your stupid help."

The contempt in Jack's voice was like the flick of a whip. Elanor's lip quivered. It made Sebastian angry. It had been a while since she'd looked so pale and anxious. She slid down to the floor and sat on the cold stone, her face bent down into her hands. The light from the ring dimmed. "Well, I won't be so stupid again."

"*You* should've told the soldiers that we had nothing to do with you," Sebastian said to Jack.

The thief shrugged. "Ah, you still may be useful to me. Maybe the lady will believe you. It's worth a try."

Sebastian felt his face grow hotter. "This is all your fault. I should have let you fall."

"I never fall."

"You were falling."

"Was not."

"Was too."

"Was not."

"You were falling. If I hadn't grabbed you, you'd have been Jack Splat."

"Another second and I'd have righted myself."
As if to underscore his meaning, Jack slowly bent
backward until one hand was touching the floor, then
he deftly shifted till all his weight was supported by
that one hand. He straightened his body, his head
down, his feet pointing to the ceiling, the other arm
stretched out to the side. He maintained this pose for
a long moment, then slowly bent his legs down till his
feet were on the floor and he could again stand. He
bowed, low, deep and mocking.

"You were falling," Sebastian insisted. "I saved
your life."

"I beg to differ."

Sebastian was so enraged, he jumped to his feet
and rushed at Jack, wanting to pummel him to the
ground. Jack swayed aside and Sebastian hit the wall
hard and was knocked down to the ground again. He
was too tired to get back up. The cell swam before his
eyes. He blinked to get his eyesight back in order.

"Would you just stop it?" Elanor said. "Things are
bad enough without you two brawling like idiots."

Jack bowed in her direction. "I'm afraid hanging

out with thugs and bullies brings out the worst in me. I do apologize, my lady."

Sebastian said nothing. He'd never felt so tired or humiliated. He couldn't look at either of them.

Elanor glared at Jack. "Last time I saw you, Jack, you were disappearing with my family silver."

"Ah, yes. Sorry about that—"

"We were attacked and you chose that moment to steal from us?"

Jack shrugged. "I'm no warrior, my lady."

Sebastian lifted his gaze then. "It was *you* who let Lord Mortlake's army into the castle, wasn't it?"

Jack's face changed.

It was only a flash, but Sebastian jumped to his feet, fists clenched. "I'm right! You traitor!"

"No, no, I didn't. I promise!"

"That's why Lord Mortlake brought you to the castle in the first place. So you could sneak around and find out how the portcullis worked and then open it for him!"

Eleanor's face was white. "So many people have been killed, my father taken prisoner, and Arwen and Mistress Pippin, too! Jack, how could you?"

"I didn't do it!"

Sebastian clenched his fists. "You sneaky little rat, I'll make you sorry!"

Jack flung up both hands. "Stop! It wasn't like that! Yes, Lord Mortlake wanted me to spy for him. That was why he brought me to the castle and put me in the pie and told me I was to pretend to be your fool. I had to sneak around and find out stuff for him, and leave the information hidden in a book in the library. I don't know who was reading it, I was never told." Jack looked nervously at Sebastian's fists, clenched so tight the knuckles were white. "But I didn't do it," Jack gabbled. "I mean, I did . . . but only once. You were so . . . kind to me, your ladyship, and Mistress Pippin too, and no one at Wolfhaven Castle mistreated me, like they did at Frostwick. I liked my new home. I was given food, and the food was good! I decided I simply wouldn't put any more notes in that book. I figured that Lord Mortlake wouldn't be able to invade if he couldn't get all the information he needed."

"But why didn't you tell us?" Elanor asked. "If only

we'd known . . ." She fell silent, twisting her fingers together. "We could have done something."

"Who'd listen to me? To a fool?" Jack said. "Besides, I was afraid you might throw me out if you knew I was a spy."

"You would have deserved it," Sebastian said.

"I didn't want to work for Lord Mortlake," Jack insisted. "I don't like him, or his horrible wife. I didn't *want* to spy for him. He made me do it. I didn't want to be anyone's *fool* either. How would you like to wear that stupid outfit?"

"Not much," Sebastian admitted.

"So what are you doing here at Crowthorne Castle?" Elanor said.

Jack shrugged and looked a little shamefaced. "Silver candlesticks and platters are hard to sell. Not many people have the funds. I'd heard Lady Ravenna was a miserly old bird who loved shiny things. I thought she might buy the silver."

"And did she?" Elanor asked.

Jack shrugged. "'Buy' is not exactly the right word. She tossed me a couple of coppers, and then, when

I protested, threatened to have me locked up in her dungeons. So I grabbed something on the way out for my trouble."

Elanor was shocked. "You stole from her!"

"She deserved it." Jack slipped his hand inside his shirt and pulled out a small drawstring bag. Opening it, he tipped a ring set with a honey-golden stone into his palm. He lifted it up and showed it to Elanor and Sebastian.

"That's amber." Sebastian touched the cloak pin fastened to his shoulder. Made of rowan wood, it was carved into the shape of a dragon, circling a smooth oval of amber. It was Sebastian's most precious belonging, given to him by Arwen.

He was sure it had some astonishing magical power that was yet to reveal itself. The talisman of the Oak King spoke to Quinn and gave her wise advice. The moonstone ring Elanor had been given conjured light. Tom's elderwood flute had summoned wolves and tamed the griffin. Sebastian was sure his gift from the Grand Teller would be just as powerful, if only he understood what to do with it.

"I bet you that's valuable," he said. "No wonder she's after you."

"Well, she shouldn't have been such a penny-pinching old miser. She took my silver, she should have paid me properly for it."

"It wasn't your silver, it was my father's," Elanor reminded him.

Jack shrugged, putting the ring away again. "If you're hoping she'll help you win back your castle, I'd think again. She won't lift a finger for you if there's not something in it for her."

Elanor looked ruefully at Sebastian. "I'm guessing we should have gone in search of the dragon after all."

Jack looked up. "Dragon?"

Sebastian grimaced at her, trying to signal that Jack couldn't be trusted with knowledge of their quest. Elanor didn't appear to notice and continued to explain. "Yes. I know it sounds ridiculous," she said, "but we've heard that a dragon guards a sacred rowan tree in the midst of the moors."

Jack laughed incredulously. "And you think you can tame it and ride it into battle?"

Sebastian's face flamed. He had indeed imagined exactly that scene many times since Arwen had sent them on their quest.

Jack's grin widened at the sight of Sebastian's face. "Good luck with that. As crazy as that sounds, it's far more likely than you persuading the old lady to cough up any coins." He slipped the drawstring bag back into his ragged tunic. "Well, it's been nice chatting about old times with you, but I must be off. I've no desire to be given to the Beast!"

"What Beast?" Sebastian demanded. Jack threw him a glance filled with mock pity.

"Oh, you'll find out soon enough." He went over to the bars and seized two in his hands.

"You think you can bend them with your bare hands?" Sebastian jeered.

Jack grinned over his shoulder, then slipped his head through the bars.

"Well, that's smart," Sebastian said. "Now you've gone and gotten your head stuck."

But Jack ignored him. He put one arm through, twisted sideways and then, somehow, managed to get one shoulder then the other through the narrow gap between the bars. As Sebastian and Elanor watched, amazed, he slowly wriggled the rest of his body through as easily as if his body was made of bindweed instead of bones.

In moments, Jack was on the far side of the cell, running across the guardroom. At the opening of the tunnel, he turned and gave Elanor and Sebastian a mocking wave. "Till we meet again!"

Sebastian ran to the bars and shook them. "Jack! You slippery eel!" he hissed, as loudly as he dared. "What Beast?!"

4

←——«« THE »»——→
GOOSE GIRL

The bare moors undulated for as far as Quinn could see, drab as old brown velvet. Here and there, the land humped into steep tors, crowned with rocky outcrops that could once have been ruined castles or the broken skulls of giants.

A pool rippled silver in one low valley, rushes bending and blowing on its shore. Quinn shivered, her arms wrapped around her legs, her chin resting on her bony knees.

"I hope nothing's gone wrong," she said in a low voice.

Tom glanced at her. "They'll be fine."

Quinn looked to the west, where the square keep

of Crowthorne Castle was silhouetted against the brightly streaked sky. "The sun's going down."

"They won't come back tonight. Lady Ravenna is sure to offer them a hot supper and a steaming bath and a soft comfy bed . . ."

At the harsh note in Tom's voice, Fergus the wolfhound whined and put one paw on his leg. Tom rubbed his rough head, gently removing the dog's paw so he would not wake the wolf cub sleeping in his lap.

"We could have gone, too," Quinn reminded him.

"Leading a unicorn and a griffin? I don't think so."

Both Tom and Quinn looked back at the little valley behind them. Quickthorn the unicorn was drinking from the brook, the water swirling around his hooves. In the dusk, he was almost invisible, his silvery-brown coat the same color as the rolling moors, his black mane and tail like the shadows cast by the gnarled branches of the old oak tree. Out here in the wild, the unicorn was camouflaged. Within the walls of a town, however, everyone would be able to see his long, sharp horn and know him for what he was.

Perched on the rocks above was Rex the griffin, gold-feathered wings folded back along his flanks, his lion ears pricked forward and fierce eagle eyes frowning. He seemed to glow in the last light as if made from burnished bronze.

There was no way to disguise such magical creatures.

"They'd have taken Rex and Quickthorn away from us," Tom said, his tone angry and impatient. "They'd never have let us keep them. Who knows what would happen to them? Chained up, most likely, put in cages, forced to fight. Sebastian is a thickhead. We should have kept to the wild, lonely places, where no one would see us and where we could keep them safe."

Quinn sighed. Although she agreed with Tom, she wished he hadn't argued so angrily with Sebastian. It only made Sebastian more stubborn. If Tom hadn't called Sebastian a pigheaded fool, maybe she and Elanor would have been able to convince him to keep away from the town. Though, she had to admit, she was hoping Elanor and Sebastian had a chance to buy them some fresh supplies. She was very tired of soup made with little more than a handful of weeds and a pinch of salt.

"We should be heading south, looking for that dragon, not sitting here, wasting time," Tom went on. "My mam's a prisoner of the bog-men and Sebastian wants to go play at the fair."

"He just wants to get some help," Quinn said. "He wants to make sure warnings are sent out to all the lords and ladies and to King Ivor so he will send an army to help Wolfhaven."

"What if Lady Ravenna refuses to help? What if she's in cahoots with Lord Mortlake?"

"What if she's not? What if she sends an army to help free your mam and Arwen and Lord Wolfgang and the rest?"

Tom grunted.

Quinn looked back at Crowthorne Castle. It cast a long shadow over the valley, hiding the town from her eyes. Sebastian and Elanor were supposed to come back before dark, yet there was no sign of them on the road, and the sky to the west was unfurling red banners of cloud. She hoped they would bring back some fresh bread and fruit and vegetables. And pork pies and sausages and jam tarts and gingerbread.

Quinn's stomach growled.

"They're probably eating roast peacock right now," Tom said. Fergus whined and laid his head down on his paws. He was hungry too, Quinn knew.

The need to hunt and forage for food had slowed the group down on their journey south. It had only grown harder once they left the Witchwood, where at least there had been plenty of wild green leaves and roots and mushrooms, and Tom had been able to shoot down wood pigeon. The moors were bare and windswept, and nothing much grew except heather and bracken and the occasional thorny patch of whortleberries. The only birds seemed to be buzzards, riding the winds far too high for arrows to reach, and although the children had once seen a herd of fallow deer, they were far too fast to catch. The moors were hard to cross as well, with bogs in every valley and rocks bursting free of the skin of the earth on every hill. They'd not dared to gallop Quickthorn, in case he broke a leg, and they had all grown very tired of being the ones to slog along on foot while Tom soared overhead on the griffin's back.

Sebastian had argued that they all should take turns riding Rex, but the griffin had made it clear that this was not an option. Whenever anyone but Tom went near him, Rex would slash at them with his sharp beak and claws, or lash out with his strong lion hindquarters. Tom couldn't hide how much the griffin's loyalty pleased him, and Sebastian couldn't hide his annoyance.

A distant honking caught Quinn's attention. She looked down the valley. A flock of white geese were waddling along the road that led from the castle. They were followed by a fair-haired girl in a smock with a long willow switch in one hand and a basket in the other.

"Maybe she would sell us some goose eggs," Quinn said. "We could scramble them up for supper."

"Good idea. Take some pennies from Mam's purse in the bottom of my bag." Tom took one hand from the back of the sleeping wolf cub and pointed at his knapsack. Quinn ran to dig the coins out.

"Remember, Fergus and Wulfric are hungry too. They haven't caught a rabbit all day," Tom said. "Buy some extra eggs for them."

Quinn ran down the hill. Another moment or two, and the goose girl and her flock would disappear around the corner.

"Stop, oh, please stop!" she cried. The rough and rocky ground hurt her bare feet, but she didn't care.

The geese heard her coming and rushed towards her, necks snaking, beaks gaping, wings flapping. Quinn threw up her arms to protect her face as they darted at her, hissing and honking.

The goose girl shouted to her. "Flap your arms and jerk your head up and down!" She demonstrated, pumping her arms up and down, thrusting her chin forward and back. Quinn stared at her in disbelief, but as the geese pecked at her legs and hands, she did as she was told. "Yah! Yah!" she shouted, flapping her arms as fast as she could. Quinn thought grimly to herself that Tom must be rolling on the ground in absolute stitches. At least Sebastian and Elanor weren't there to see her acting like a goose, though she had no doubt Tom would describe the scene to them later.

The flapping and chin poking worked, and the geese backed away from her, beaks gaping. Quinn was able to drop her arms and lift her skirts to look down at her legs, already empurpling with bruises.

"I'm so sorry!" The goose girl hurried to her side. She looked about eighteen or nineteen years old. "There was such a kerfuffle at the market today, and it's made them very irritable."

"A kerfuffle? What happened?" Quinn's voice was sharp with anxiety, her thoughts leaping to Sebastian and Elanor at once.

"Some thieves were arrested."

"Thieves? What for? What did they look like?"

The goose girl looked at her in surprise. "One was a skinny dark-haired boy, slippery as an eel. It was he who upset the geese, and broke all my eggs."

Quinn relaxed in relief, but the goose girl went on. "But I spoke with the cartwright afterwards. He was coming out of the castle when they caught two more thieves up near there. There was another boy—

a redhead. There was a girl as well, a skinny little thing in a green dress. They were all working together, the cartwright said."

Quinn gasped, her hand flying up to her mouth.

"Why? Do you know them?" The goose girl straightened her back, her voice angry.

"No, no, of course not," Quinn gabbled. "What . . . what happened to them?"

"The cartwright said they were dragged off to the dungeons. Lady Ravenna cannot abide thieves. They'll be condemned and given to the bog tomorrow."

Quinn was aghast. "Given to the bog? What do you mean?"

"It's Harvest Day tomorrow," the goose girl answered. "That's the day of executions. Then the bodies are thrown into the bog."

"But . . . that's barbaric! Why would you not bury them decently?"

The goose girl narrowed her eyes in suspicion, but Quinn was too upset to hide her feelings. Elanor and Sebastian condemned! *It must be some kind of mistake*, she thought. *Perhaps they pretended to be thieves as some kind of ruse to get in and see Lady Ravenna?* And the bog! Arwen had always taught her that every person was entitled to burial rites. To throw them in the bog, like rubbish . . .

Take care, little maid, a voice spoke in her mind. *This is an old dark place with old dark ways.*

"Where are you from?" the goose girl asked abruptly. "You can't be from around here, else you'd know about the Harvest Day executions. Everyone here knows about the bog."

"Oh, no, I'm not," Quinn said, feeling herself redden. "I'm . . . I'm from . . . up north." She waved her hand in a generally northern direction. "We're just traveling through. I saw you and . . . I wanted to buy some eggs from you."

The goose girl scowled. "I've not got a single egg left. That thief smashed them all. I wasn't able to sell one."

A shadow crossed her face and she stood silent for a moment, frowning. Then she smiled with an effort and looked up at Quinn. "But I have more at home. Plenty of them. You're welcome to a few, to say sorry for my geese pecking you."

Quinn hesitated. She wanted to rush back to Tom and tell him about the thieves that were taken and her fear that Sebastian and Elanor were in trouble. She began to shake her head, but the goose girl said insistently, "Oh, but you must! It's not right to let you go off with your legs all bitten and bruised like that. My cottage is just around the corner. I'll give you some ham to go with your eggs, and some apple and whortleberry pie."

That did sound good. Quinn was very hungry.

Tongue of silver and hair of gold, hide feet of clay and heart of stone, the voice said in Quinn's mind. She closed her hand over the medallion she wore around her neck. It had been carved from ancient bog oak into the semblance of an old man's face, with fronds of leaves instead of hair.

Sometimes he spoke to her. Many times the Oak King's words were wise; many other times they had seemed to make little sense. Quinn was too tired and too hungry now to try and make sense of his riddles. She wanted to concentrate on the goose girl's words.

"I have fresh bread too," the goose girl said. "It's delicious with jam. And my grandmother will have roast goose pie in the larder. I'll gladly give you a few slices."

Quinn glanced back up the hill. She thought about how hungry she and Tom were, and how there was nothing left to eat in their packs. She nodded. "I can't be gone long though; it's getting dark."

Darker still it will get before the night is done, the Oak King said.

Shhh, Quinn thought, and flushed as she realized her lips had moved and the goose girl had seen. "I'm afraid of getting lost after dark," she said quickly. "There are so few landmarks on the moors."

The goose girl looked concerned. "You aren't camping on the moors, are you? It's not safe. You could sprain your ankle on the rocks or fall down a cleft, or be pixy led into the bog. You don't want to go in there. The Beast will get you."

"The Beast?" Quinn's heart quickened.

"You don't know about the Beast? Why, now I know you're a stranger. The Beast lives in the bog and will snatch anyone foolish enough to stray there."

"What kind of beast?" Quinn clasped her hands together in hope. "A dragon?"

"Oh no, the dragons are all long gone," the goose girl answered. "Nothing but their bones left. No, this beast is something else. Something huge and black and hairy. He comes prowling around whenever he is hungry. He'll take any living thing he can get his claws on . . . chicken or goat or pig. I hear him often, howling at the moon."

Quinn shivered. She wrapped her arms around her body.

"Oh, I'm sorry," the goose girl said. "I didn't mean to scare you. It's not the time or the place for beast stories. Not with the dark coming on. Come, let's hurry home and I'll pack you a basket of goodies."

She set off down the road, driving the geese before

her with her willow switch. Quinn followed along behind. She felt uneasy leaving behind Tom and the animals, but the offer of food was too good to be passed up. And the goose girl seemed nice enough, if you paid no heed to her stories.

Surely it would only take a few minutes.

5

SEARCHING ▸▸→ ▸▸→ THE MOORS

Tom stood, the wind whipping his hair away from his face, gazing down the road. The sun had already sunk away, and twilight was deepening over the bare, rolling hills. Where could Quinn be? She'd been gone for so long. Surely she wouldn't have gone far?

Tom paced up and down. He had already walked ten minutes or more up the road, calling her name till his throat was hoarse, but there was no sound, nor sight of any house or path. Eventually he'd returned to the campsite, hoping he'd somehow missed her and she was sitting there, cooking them some supper.

Stars were beginning to burn in the east, and a

huge blood-colored moon sat on the horizon. The unicorn was uneasy, fretting back and forth and neighing occasionally, his black mane blowing in the wind.

Tom couldn't bear it. "Stay here," he said to the wolfhound and wolf cub. He put his longbow and quiver of arrows over his shoulder, then grabbed his flute from his pocket. Made of elder wood, it was slim and crooked, with a wooden bird perched near the mouthpiece.

He played a quick tune on it and the griffin perched on the rocks spread his golden wings and flew down to Tom. He landed lightly beside Tom, head cocked.

"Ready to fly, Rex?" Tom asked and leapt up onto the griffin's back. "Let's go!"

The griffin soared into the sky as Quickthorn neighed from the dark below. Leaning over his shoulder, Tom could see the moonlit moors stretching as far as the eye could see. They were eerily empty. No lights, no houses, no people. No Quinn.

On he flew. The moon slowly rose and shrunk. The stars brightened. The moors became a cloth of silver, embroidered with strange black designs. Tom swooped back towards Crowthorne Castle.

As the griffin flew over a fold of the moor, Tom glimpsed a smudge of what looked like smoke far below. He flew down and saw the low shape of a cottage huddled into a bare ridge. The faintest edge of light showed through the crack of a shutter. Tom could smell the smoke now, and, as he flew lower, the delicious aroma of a meal cooking. His stomach growled. He was giddy with hunger.

As the griffin flew down to the cottage, a sudden hissing like a thousand snakes rose from the dark garden. Rex swerved away, startled. Tom saw large white shapes like ghosts rushing at him from all directions. He urged the griffin higher. The ghostly shapes flapped after him, but soon fell away. Tom's heart was pounding. Then he heard a familiar honking sound.

He realized the shapes were, in fact, geese. He had found the goose girl's cottage.

He wheeled Rex around and flew back down to the cottage. A door opened and a wedge of light cut into the darkness. "What is it, geese? What do you hear?" a girl's voice cried. The geese honked loudly in response. Tom heard another voice from inside the cottage. *If that's Quinn*, he thought grimly, *I'll be furious! Sitting around and enjoying supper while I'm flying around searching for her . . .*

Tom guided Rex down and dropped from the griffin's back onto the roof. He landed with a great rustle on the thatched reeds. The geese honked loudly. Immediately he hunkered down, while the griffin silently soared away.

"What is up with those geese tonight?" the goose girl said. Tom could hear her quite clearly for he was crouched near the hole in the roof above the hearth-pit, where the smoke from the fire drifted out. The goose girl unlocked the door and came out into the garden again, looking up at the roof. "Shoo! Get down from there."

The geese honked loudly and some flew away. Tom pressed himself flat against the thatch, hoping the goose girl would not see him. She seemed satisfied, going back inside the cottage and shutting the door. He heard a bolt being drawn.

"Perhaps it's the Beast?" another voice quavered. She sounded old and tired.

"He has no need to hunt tonight," the goose girl said. "I gave him the girl. I left her bound to the rowan tree."

Was she talking about Quinn? A chill ran down Tom's body. He could scarcely believe what he was hearing.

Panic seized him. He had to find out what the goose girl meant. Tom slid down the thatch and landed in the dark garden below. The geese rushed him at once, but he kicked them away and ran to the door of the cottage. It was locked and barred. He battered at it with his fists and feet, then threw his body against it. From inside he heard shrieks of fear.

"It's the Beast!"

"Go away!"

Tom couldn't break the door down. Barely thinking, he tried wrenching a shutter off one of the low windows, but it was securely fastened. "Go away!" the goose girl screamed again.

Tom dragged the flute from his pocket and tried to call the griffin to him. He could hardly drag in a breath, his chest was so tight with fear for Quinn. At last he managed to play a few shaky notes. In a few wing beats, the griffin was by Tom's side, and he tore the door from the cottage with his strong talons.

Tom burst in, his longbow armed and lifted, the griffin shrieking with rage at his shoulder. "Where is she? Where's Quinn?"

The cottage was dark and smoky. A fire smoldered on the dirt floor, a black pot hanging above it on a tripod made of sticks. An old woman had fallen off a wooden stool and crouched on the floor, sobbing.

"Please, don't hurt us," the goose girl screamed. She shrank back in terror from the sight of the great beast with his gaping beak and raking claws.

Tom turned to the griffin. "Go, Rex!"

The griffin beat his huge golden wings and rose

fluidly into the air. In a moment, he had disappeared into the darkness again.

"You're not the Beast! Who are you?" the goose girl demanded.

"What have you done with Quinn?" Tom demanded.

"Who? Oh! The girl—"

"Where is she?" Tom lifted his bow.

"Please, no . . . I'm sorry . . . I had to—"

"Where is she?" Tom spoke through his teeth.

"I took her to the Beast . . . he lives up in the bog."

"But why?"

"Because she knows those thieves that broke all my eggs!" the goose girl burst out. "I didn't earn a cent today, and now we'll starve! She's a thief too, I know it!"

Tom could hardly understand what it was the goose girl had told him.

"You've given Quinn to some beast in the bog? What for? To eat?"

"Not to eat, not to eat." The goose girl cowered away from him.

"What will he do to her then?"

"He'll kill her, then give her body to the bog at midday," the old woman answered in a shaky voice.

Tom could not hold his bow up any longer. His arms and legs felt weak. He stumbled forward, gripping on to the edge of the table with both hands. "How could you do such a thing?" he whispered. "Couldn't you have gone to the castle, to ask for your lady's help? Surely a battalion of soldiers could kill this Beast?"

She stared at him uncomprehendingly. "It's his job!"

Tom stared back at her. Slowly understanding dawned. "You mean, the lady knows about this beast? She knows he's throwing people into the bog?"

They all nodded.

"It's always been so," the old woman said. "For as far back as anyone can remember."

"It's his job, as it was his father's and his grandfather's," the goose girl said.

"And the bog must be appeased." The old woman stood up slowly, one hand at her back, her face screwed up in pain. "Once there was a grand castle up on the moors, by the shore of a shining stretch of lake, but it was all sucked down into the bog and now nothing is left but a few ruins. If we do not give the bog offerings, it could swallow the whole moor."

Tom frowned, a faint memory stirring. He was sure he had heard a story like that recently.

"They take the condemned prisoners from the Crowthorne dungeons to him," the goose girl said. "Four times a year, at every Fire Festival. They must be punished, mustn't they? The Lady must keep law and order in her lands. The Beast carries out their sentence and then he throws them in the bog." A look of sudden malice twisted her pretty face. "That's why I took her. She knew those thieves that stole all my eggs and broke them. She tried to pretend that she didn't, but I could tell. Birds of a feather flock together, everyone knows that. So she's a thief, too! The Beast would have had her in the end. What harm does it do to hand her over before he looks for her? Else they would have thought I helped her, and I would have been given to the bog as well!"

Tom was so puzzled he could only stare at her.

"They were taken in the marketplace," the goose girl continued impatiently. "That big boy with the red hair and the girl in the green gown. They helped that wicked boy who smashed all my eggs and so were arrested too. They're in prison now. Serves them right."

Tom had to sit down. His legs were shaking. Sebastian and Elanor had been thrown into prison?

"It was their fault I lost all my eggs. Your friend's, too. Why should I pay the price for helping her? Tomorrow, they'll be punished properly. They'll all be thrown in the bog!"

6

THE →
→BEAST

Quinn sat hunched, in darkness, tied tightly to the rowan tree with apron strings. Her hands throbbed and her wrists stung where the bonds cut into her skin. She tried again to wrench herself free, but cried out in pain. She couldn't move at all.

Quinn had always prided herself on her insight into people, but the goose girl had been so young and pretty and seemingly sweet. Quinn had followed her willingly, even when she had turned off the road and led her down a narrow twisting path into the moors. She had been hungry, and eager for the basket of goodies the goose girl had promised. Quinn could have kicked herself for being such a fool.

Sylvan had kept muttering about things dark and old, wicked and cold, yet still Quinn followed. Then the goose girl led Quinn up a steep hill to what looked like the ruin of a great castle, looming high on a rocky tor. The long twilight had begun to fade into dark. Quinn's anxiety had grown, but the goose girl had turned, and smiled, and beckoned her on. "Almost there now."

Quinn had smelled peat smoke and the homey smell had reassured her. She had followed the goose girl into the shadowy ruins, through a cavernous arched tunnel and into a wide valley filled with bog. It stretched for miles, brown and flat, between steep hills crowned with outcrops of boulders, huge against the dimming sky. In the center of the bog was another steep hill, rising like an island out of the stretches of water and mud and waving grasses.

A surge of excitement ran through Quinn's veins as she recognized the feathery leaves of an ancient rowan tree, growing at the peak of the island. Its foam of white flowers was already quickening to berries, petals blowing away in the breeze. Its trunk was thick and twisted, all bent over from the wind, its branches reaching out like a shrieking girl. On its far side, a large flat rock jutted out over the bog.

"The rowan tree," Quinn had breathed. "Can we go to it?"

"Of course," the goose girl had said. "There is a secret path through the bog. Follow me."

Together they had stumbled through the mire, following a faint and winding path that led from one small mossy clump to a fallen log to an island of rushes to a sunken wooden plank. Both lurched off the path more than once and found themselves up to their knees in sucking mud. Quinn barely noticed. All of her being was focused on that rowan tree and the hope that she might—somehow, crazily, impossibly—find the dragon of legend curled around its roots.

What she had seen when at last she struggled, muddy and exhausted, up onto the island, had almost brought her to her knees. It had been easy enough for the goose girl to order her flock to attack her. It had been easy enough—in the mad storm of white feathers and snapping beaks—for the goose girl to bind her to the tree with her apron strings.

All Quinn had been able to see was the enormous skull of a dragon, lying bleached and broken in the grass.

Tears stung her eyes at the memory. It had been a fool's errand, looking for a dragon. An impossible task. And now she and her friends were all separated and she was trussed as neatly as a hen ready for market. Quinn tried once again to reach her little witch's knife, made of sharp black obsidian glass, but her wrists were bound too tightly. "Help!" she cried into the night. The wind rustling through the rowan tree's branches was her only reply. The tears tracked down her wind-stung cheeks. "Help!"

Shush, little maid, Sylvan said urgently. Quinn fell silent. She could hear something large swishing towards her through the rushes. Then a huge shadow reared over her. Quinn screamed. A hand clapped over her mouth. Something sharp slashed through her bonds. Then she was lifted and flung over a broad shoulder. A grunt. Rough hair under her hands. A lurching walk, crashing through the rushes. Quinn tried to scream and struggle, but whatever carried her was far too strong.

The Beast! she thought. *The Beast has got me!*

THE LADY OF
CROWTHORNE
← «CASTLE» →

Sebastian and Elanor stood in the prison cell, listening to Jack's swift feet disappear down the passageway. Then Elanor sat down again, burying her face in her arms. Once again the light of her moonstone ring faded away, till it was only the faintest shimmer on her clenched hand.

It was icy in the dungeons. Sebastian had to clench his teeth to stop them from chattering uncontrollably. It might be high summer, with twilight lingering for hours, but here in the prison it was eternal winter, eternal night.

Sebastian cupped his hand over his dragon brooch. Dragons meant fire and gold and revenge. Surely he could conjure flames to warm them and light their way. Surely he could blast their way free. He rubbed his brooch, he breathed on it, he pressed it against his heart, his pulse, he pleaded with it.

Nothing happened. The amber warmed under his touch, but there was no blaze, no bonfire, no change. Finally Sebastian could do no more but slide down to sit on the floor, his head bowed.

He could hear Elanor sniffling.

"I wish we'd stopped to buy some food," Sebastian said at last. "I am so hungry."

"I thought Lady Ravenna would welcome us and feed us, not throw us in the dungeon."

Sebastian bit his lip, then said gruffly, "I'm sorry, it's my fault."

"I'm the one who asked you to save Jack," she answered, wiping her nose on her silken sleeve.

"Yes, but I was the one who made us come here in the first place . . ."

"Let's not argue about whose fault it is," Elanor cried angrily, then stopped and laughed. "Ladies never argue."

There was a moment when neither spoke, then she bent and breathed softly on her ring. Light flickered up again. Neither could meet the other's gaze.

"What are we going to do?" Sebastian said.

"What *can* we do? We'll wait and hopefully Lady Ravenna will want to see us and we can convince her of the truth of our story."

Sebastian sighed.

The sound of running feet made them jump up and rush to the bars. Jack sprinted out of the tunnel.

"What are you doing?" Sebastian called.

Jack put one finger to his mouth and then dived under the table, crouching in its shadow. The sound of marching boots. Light flickered down the tunnel. Elanor gasped and wrenched her shining ring off her finger, thrusting it into her pocket so its radiance was snuffed.

Then came the soldiers in their black-and-white livery. *One, two, three, four, left, right, stand!*

"Right, you lot, her ladyship wants to see you," the troop leader said, fitting the key into the lock. He opened the gate and only then realized that there were only two prisoners in the cell instead of three.

He stared around, openmouthed, his expression gradually darkening as he realized Jack was gone.

"Where'd he go? How did he get out?" the troop leader shouted.

"He just squeezed through the bars and ran away," Elanor said. "I've never seen anything like it."

"Where did he go?" The troop leader's face was scarlet, his eyes bulging.

Sebastian swallowed. He saw Elanor's quick, pleading glance and felt the presence of Jack crouching under the table like a burning ember in the corner of his eye. He could not believe the soldiers did not see Jack, or hear his ragged, uneven breathing. For a moment, he wavered. There would be a certain satisfaction in seeing Jack dragged out and put in chains.

But Sebastian could not forget the desperate clutch of the other boy's hand in his, in that muscle-shrieking, joint-tearing moment when Jack had swung away from the cliff, a hundred feet of space yawning below him.

Sebastian looked down at the ground so he would not betray Jack with an involuntary glance in his direction. "He ran that way," he said, pointing towards the tunnel.

"That boy is as slimy as a snake," the troop leader said. For a moment he stood, head lowered, jaw working. "Her ladyship will not be pleased," he muttered, before looking up and issuing a swift set of orders. "Right, you lot, turn this guardhouse upside down and find me that boy! You two, come with me. Don't think of trying any tricks, else I'll have the hide off you."

Sebastian tried hard not to let his eyes flick towards Jack, hiding under the table. He hoisted his pack onto his back and walked out of the cell. Elanor kept close to his side, her face all scrunched up in anxiety. Together they followed the troop leader back along the tunnel, and began the long climb up to the castle keep.

At last they were led into the great hall, a dark and cavernous building with heavy hammer beams arching overhead. Up at the far end was a huge fireplace, with a tiny fire smoldering inside. A long wooden table stood before it, a single candelabra shedding soft, unstable light over a great array of glittering silver objects. Sebastian saw platters, bowls, goblets, jugs, trays, sugar bowls, spoons, ladles, carving knives, jewelry boxes, figurines, all neatly arranged in rows. A small woman in a black dress sat on a bench, carefully rubbing a silver cup. Her hair was tucked up under a cloth and she wore a long tarnish-streaked apron. She looked up as Sebastian and Elanor approached. Thin and white and pinched, her face was dominated by a large, beaky nose and two snapping, black eyes.

She must be the housekeeper, Sebastian thought, and wondered why she was cleaning the silver up in the great hall instead of down in the kitchen.

"Have you no manners?" she cried, in a rusty-sounding voice. "Make your bow to me, knave!"

The troop leader slapped Sebastian hard on the back of the head. Taken by surprise, he stumbled forward but managed to recover and made a clumsy bow.

"So this is supposed to be the Lord of Ashbyrne's

son? He can't even make a decent bow!" The old woman glared at him. He tried again and managed a better bow and Elanor quickly sank into a curtsey.

"So you're claiming to be the Lord of Wolfhaven's daughter? Look at you! Your hair's a bird's nest, your clothes are a disgrace, you look like you've been dragged through a hedge. Have you never been taught the proper way to approach a lady?"

"I … I'm sorry, your ladyship," Elanor stammered. "Please forgive me coming into your presence in such a state. It was unavoidable. We have no luggage, no change of clothes, no one to help us. You see, my father—"

"Enough! You think I believe your tall tale? As if the Lord of Wolfhaven would ever allow his precious daughter to rampage around the country dressed like a hoyden, her skirts in tatters and holes in her shoes. No, you are frauds, tricksters, hustlers. You seek to swindle me, but I'm up to your tricks. You shan't fleece me."

"But, your ladyship, I promise! My father—"

"Your father is probably some wellborn scoundrel fallen on hard times but able at least to teach you a few pretty court manners that you think are enough to pull the wool over my eyes. Well, let me tell you, you good-for-nothing ruffian, I'm up to your tricks!"

Elanor pulled herself upright. "I am Lady Elanor de Belleterre, daughter of the Lord of Wolfhaven Castle, and our people have been taken! If you do not listen to me, you suspicious old bat, you could well be the next to fall!"

Sebastian gaped at her. He had never heard Elanor speak with such ringing conviction, or, for that matter, so rudely.

The head trooper gaped at her.

Lady Ravenna gaped at her.

Elanor spoke into the stunned silence. "My home has been invaded and my father and all his people killed or captured. Lord Mortlake betrayed us and called upon the foulest black magic to do so. We have come here to beg for your help." She clasped both hands together. "We need to send word to the other lords of the High Marches and to the King. All we ask of you is paper and ink and messengers with fast horses."

"And who, pray tell, shall pay for that paper and ink, and the messengers' wages and the horses' oats? Who shall pay for the bribes to smooth the messengers' passage and for the beds they must sleep in, the food they must eat?"

"My father would pay you back!"

"Yet did you not say your father is enslaved, his castle captured, all his people seized? How can he pay me back when he's a slave?"

"He won't stay a slave!" Sebastian shouted. Elanor threw him a grateful glance. "We're going to rescue him! And all our friends, too!"

"Really? How?"

Sebastian's hand rose to touch his dragon brooch. "We'll find the way."

The old woman's eyes flickered to his brooch and instinctively he covered it, hiding it from her gaze.

"I know the other lords would rise to my father's defense," Elanor said, "for are you not friends and allies? Would not my father come to your rescue if you were the one invaded? The King himself bade you all to stand strong and work together. What would King

Ivor think if word came to him that you refused to help us? That you knew of betrayal and black magic in the land you are sworn to protect, yet had done nothing?"

The old woman stared down at her neat rows of gleaming silver, her thin mouth compressed, her fingers clutched together. Then she raised her eyes, fixing her black gaze upon them.

"I suppose a messenger is not too much to ask. It's not like you want an army. An army costs a lot to feed. An army gets restless if it's not paid. But a messenger . . . what's a single man and a horse?"

Elanor and Sebastian exchanged a single exultant glance, though Sebastian could not help thinking they should have argued for an army. At least a battalion or two. He imagined himself riding back to Wolfhaven Castle at the head of an army, raising his arm, commanding them to charge. His father would be so proud. "Valor, glory, victory!" was his family's war cry. Sebastian imagined shouting it and the roar of a thousand voices responding, the thunder of four thousand hooves, the clang of swords and shields, the hiss of arrows, the moan of defeat as the enemy fell.

He imagined Elanor's admiring glance.

"I suppose I can spare a single man," Lady Ravenna said. "And a pony. Or maybe a donkey."

Elanor's forehead creased. She shot a look of worry at Sebastian.

"But I must have surety," Lady Ravenna continued. "Some kind of insurance, in case your father does not win back his castle."

"But . . . we have nothing. What could we give you?" Elanor waved her hands down her ruined skirts, her worn-out shoes.

Lady Ravenna smiled. "Your squire can give me his amber brooch. My own ring has been stolen and I miss it. It's the only thing of value I can see. Give me the brooch and I'll bear the cost of sending out a messenger."

Sebastian swallowed. He sent a quick glance at Elanor. Her eyes pleaded with him. Slowly he reached up and unpinned the dragon brooch, rubbing his thumb over the smooth oval of amber. It seemed to warm under his touch. He stared at it, then at Lady Ravenna's avaricious face. Surely Arwen's gift was meant for more than this, a cheap bargain made with an even cheaper crone? But they had nothing more to bargain with. With another swift glance at Elanor, Sebastian reluctantly held the brooch out to Lady Ravenna. She snatched it from his hand, gloating.

"Sir Oliver, find me a messenger. And a mule."

MOLDY »——→
←——« CHEESE

Elanor sat at the table and looked down at the plate that had just been dropped in front of her. It contained a hunk of old black bread and some moldy cheese, nothing else.

"That's all there is, I'm sorry," said the maid. "With the feast tomorrow, her ladyship doesn't want to be spending any more than she needs to. That's all we've got as well."

The maid was small and skinny and she was dressed in a shabby brown gown, several sizes too small for her, with wooden clogs on her feet. She looked like a field worker, not a servant in one of the great castles of Stormness.

"I'm sorry I can't light a fire for you, but it's strictly forbidden," the maid went on.

"Any chance of a hot bath?" Elanor asked hopefully.

She made a face. "Sorry. I can bring up a pitcher of warm water for you."

"What about some fresh clothes?" Elanor looked down at her filthy torn green silk.

The maid hesitated. "I can bring you up a needle and thread. Lady Ravenna would not approve of me giving you any old clothes. She sells them all."

She bobbed a curtsey and walked away, leaving Elanor alone in a bare room high in one of the towers. There was a bed with a patched counterpane, a wooden stool and a table. A moth-eaten rug lay on the stone floor. The cobwebbed hearth looked like a fire had not been laid there in centuries.

Elanor peered out an arrow slit in the wall. All she could see was the lonely high moors under a darkening sky. She wondered if Tom and Quinn had been able to catch something to eat. They were probably gorging on roast rabbit right now, sitting and laughing around a fire.

Elanor wished they had not all argued so much that morning. She wished they had all stayed together.

It was a while before the maid came back, with a jug of lukewarm water in one hand and a basin in the other. "I'm sorry I was so long. Visitors have just arrived and they want food and wine and the best bedchambers aired. We've all been thrown into such a tizzy. Her ladyship has ordered roast pheasant!"

She put down the jug and basin, slopping water everywhere in her haste. "Sorry, I have to run." With another quick curtsey, she clattered out of the room.

Roast pheasant did sound good! Elanor thought. She had managed to nibble some of the bread and cheese, but it had been awful and she was still ravenously hungry. Elanor looked at the dress on the bed, then back at her plate. Anger lit her. Lady Ravenna would not banish her, Lady Elanor of Wolfhaven Castle, to a meal of moldy cheese while she feasted on roast pheasant. She marched over to the bowl and was glad to find a small slither of soap inside it. She stripped off her tattered dress, poured out some lukewarm water and had a good wash. She found a comb on the bedside table and managed to force it through the knots in her hair till it was smooth and shiny again. Then she sponged down her dress and sewed up the worst of the tears. She could hear Mistress Mauldred's voice in her head: *Look how large those stitches are, Lady Elanor! Pluck them out and do it again. A lady's stitches should be invisible!*

Elanor dressed and braided her long golden-brown hair, then went across to the door. She was about to open it when she heard a sound outside, like hurried breathing. Elanor's heart began to thump. She opened the door unexpectedly and someone fell into the room.

It was Sebastian.

"What are you doing?" Elanor demanded.

"I was looking for you. I wanted to make sure you were all right."

"I'm hungry."

"Me too! I thought we might go in search of some proper food."

"The maid told me Lady Ravenna has ordered roast pheasant for her supper!"

"Fancy ordering a feast for herself and giving us moldy cheese and stale bread! Let's go and invite ourselves to the feast."

Determined, the pair marched along the corridor. Sebastian had washed and tidied himself too, Elanor noticed. His red velvet coat had been sponged clean, his knee-high boots polished. Even his red hair had been brushed down neatly.

Elanor and Sebastian made no attempt to be inconspicuous as they went down the stairs, but the closer they came to the great hall, the slower and more quietly they moved. They could hear voices echoing up the stairwell. Then they heard a high, tinkling laugh.

Sebastian and Elanor came to an abrupt halt. They knew that laugh. They looked at each other in absolute shock, then tiptoed down a side hall to the minstrel's gallery that overlooked the hall. A tapestry curtain hung across the doorway. Very carefully, Sebastian parted the curtain and both peeked through.

Only a few candles had been lit on the table and mantelpiece. Firelight cast a warm glow into the gloom and outlined a slim figure in red silk who stood on the hearth, warming her hands. Black hair hung like a curtain down her back.

Elanor stifled a squeak.

It was Lady Mortlake.

"These old castles are so damp and draughty, aren't they?" she said in her sweet, melodious voice. "I don't know why we live in them. Personally, of course, I'd be happy with a modern manor house, but my husband is terribly attached to his old pile and will not consider leaving."

"Is that so?" Lady Ravenna said. "I heard Frostwick Castle is practically falling down around your ears."

Lady Mortlake stiffened. "Oh, it's not quite that bad. A little shabby, yes, but falling down . . ." Her laugh tinkled out. "You really must not listen to malicious gossip, my dear Lady Ravenna."

"I am glad to hear it, because I'm afraid I have had to review our little . . . hmmm . . . business arrangement."

Elanor turned to Sebastian and mouthed, "I told you so."

Lady Mortlake frowned. "What? No! I need more bog-men. Harvest Day is tomorrow. I need the ritual Harvest fire to raise the bog-men, and I cannot wait three months for another Fire Festival if we miss it!" She stamped one small foot.

"But what on earth are you using all these poor dead souls for?" Lady Ravenna asked, pretending to be piously shocked.

Lady Mortlake showed her teeth in a smile. "Now, now. We agreed it was better for you *not* to know."

"Well, yes. But word has come to me that you and your husband have been involved in . . . shall we say . . . some property expansion?"

Elanor ground her teeth in rage. How dare Lady Ravenna call the invasion of her homeland mere *property expansion*. People had died! Her father and friends were enslaved!

"Ah, you have been listening to gossip," Lady Mortlake replied, sharply. "May I ask where you heard such news?"

"I have my sources," Lady Ravenna said. "You realize, of course, that this changes everything. If King

Ivor should hear that your dear husband has invaded his neighbor, one of the lords of the High Marches, he will be extremely displeased." She paused, then said, lingering over the words: "*Extremely* displeased."

Lady Mortlake tried to laugh. "But the King is so far away! And so busy with his own concerns. A minor squabble between neighbors need not concern him."

"Unrest on the Marches would concern him very much." Lady Ravenna took up a cloth and began polishing a two-handled silver cup. "Ah, poor King Ivor. He has never sat easily on his throne. Such bad luck . . . First losing his brother, King Gwydion. Then *both* his nephews, King Conway and King Derwyn . . . dead within a few years of each other! That's a lot of dead kings. And amongst it all, poor King Ivor, left to manage the kingdom. And still no heir to the throne!"

Lady Ravenna paused, holding the silver cup to the light, admiringly.

"There are some who say he killed King Derwyn to seize the throne himself—though of course *I* would *never* believe such a terrible thing," she added. "Nonetheless, in this part of the world, where so many can claim kinship to the royal family, you can understand why King Ivor always suspects rebellion and treason. I seem to remember Lord Mortlake was some kind of cousin to King Ivor—"

Lady Mortlake tried to smile. "Oh, my dear, no! Third cousin, twice removed. Nothing more than that."

"Your father-in-law was King Ivor's cousin. That means your husband is the king's first cousin, once removed. I do like to study genealogy tables, you know. And I believe I am right in assuming that the King will not be happy to discover that his cousin's son has invaded and conquered land with a river and a harbor and a fleet of ships now, will he?"

All pretense of a smile had fled. Lady Mortlake looked slit eyed and dangerous as she heard the veiled threat in Lady Ravenna's words. "There's no need for him to know. And I am sure I can rely on your discretion, Lady Ravenna. After all, the creatures that invaded Wolfhaven Castle came from *your* bog."

There was silence as Lady Ravenna began to polish her cup again. "Well, yes, that is true, isn't it? Not that I knew what use you had for my poor bog-men, conjured from their swampy graves. Nonetheless, I cannot allow you to conjure any more."

"I'll double the price!" Lady Mortlake shouted.

Lady Ravenna pursed her lips, looking at herself in the gleaming side of the silver cup.

"I'll triple it!" Lady Mortlake cried. After a brief pause, she said, "Fine, I'll *quadruple* it!"

"It's such a pleasure doing business with you," Lady Ravenna said, holding out her hand.

Lady Mortlake sighed, got out her purse and began to count coins into the old woman's hand.

BUSINESS TRANSACTIONS

"We have to escape," Sebastian whispered. "If Lady Mortlake realizes we're here . . ."

Elanor nodded. "There must be a back way out."

The two were creeping away from the gallery when they heard the march of soldiers' boots. They quickly hid themselves in the folds of the curtains.

"Lady Ravenna, we've caught that dratted thief again. The little ruffian was down in the dungeons, setting all the prisoners free!"

"What!" Lady Ravenna started to her feet, her black eyes snapping. "Who shall we give to the bog at noon tomorrow, if we have no prisoners?"

"They all escaped, every one of them. We got him,

though. For some reason, he came back. Probably looking for something else to steal."

"Bring him in!"

Elanor peeked through the crack in the curtain as the soldiers dragged Jack Spry into the great hall. He was dripping wet and shivering, his black curls plastered to his face, a puddle forming around his bare feet. He was flanked on all sides by grinning soldiers in black-and-white livery.

"We caught him slithering up the sewer pipe! He must've been lost, he was going the wrong way!" The soldiers all laughed.

"Stop!" Lady Mortlake came forward in an indignant swirl of red skirts. "I know this boy! He's in my employ!"

"Then, perhaps, you can explain what he's doing, sneaking and thieving his way around my castle?"

"I don't know! I thought he was . . ." Lady Mortlake suddenly shut her mouth.

"Yes?" Lady Ravenna asked.

The black-haired lady did not speak, frowning and tapping one long fingernail against her red-stained mouth.

Lady Ravenna turned her attention to Jack. "Have you searched him? Found anything?"

The troop leader smiled grimly and held out the amber ring. Lady Ravenna pounced on it, smiling, and shoved it back on her gnarled finger. "Wonderful. This is proving to be a most pleasant–and profitable– evening." She turned back to Lady Mortlake. "So, this filthy little thief is in your employ. Is he spying on me?"

"Of course not." Lady Mortlake sounded nervous.

"Well, I guess I have two choices. I can choose to disbelieve you and have him taken to my dungeon where my men will force all his secrets out of him. They have very effective methods, I assure you. Then, tomorrow, he'll be condemned and thrown in the bog, which is what we do with thieves around here."

Both Lady Mortlake and Jack turned white. Jack looked at the door, then at the arrow slits, and finally cast a desperate glance up at the minstrel's gallery. Elanor jerked back, afraid he would see her peeking through the curtain.

"Or . . ." Lady Ravenna paused.

"Or?" Lady Mortlake echoed.

"Or I could believe you and surrender the boy into your care."

"Well, that seems the best solution, doesn't it?" Lady Mortlake smiled.

"Perhaps. I shall, of course, expect payment for all the trouble he has caused me."

Lady Mortlake's smile stiffened. "Of course."

Lady Ravenna waited. After a long moment, Lady Mortlake brought out her purse once more and counted some silver coins into the old woman's greedily outstretched hand. She stopped, but Lady Ravenna did not put her hand away. Reluctantly, Lady Mortlake added more.

"Surely we must be ready for dinner now." Lady Ravenna dropped the coins into her heavy purse with a satisfied smile. "Doing business always makes me hungry."

Lady Mortlake jerked her head in agreement. Her smile was stiff and false.

"But first," murmured another voice, "there's another small matter to address." Elanor leaned forward, as a ragged old figure hobbled out of the shadows.

"Wilda?" she whispered, panicked. Sebastian's eyes widened. He hurriedly shushed her.

It was Wilda, the witch of the Witchwood. Last time Elanor and Sebastian had seen her, her blind eyes were milky white. Now her eyes were as clear and blue as a child's. She was still hunched over as cruelly as ever, leaning heavily on her staff.

Elanor and Sebastian shrank back into the shadows. It was a shock to see the old witch here. Wilda had helped them escape Lord Mortlake's forces in the forest; she had risked her own life to save them. What was she doing here with the enemy? Was she in danger?

"There are four children," Wilda said, "in company with a unicorn and a griffin, last seen heading this way. They are thieves and troublemakers. They stole the unicorn from my lady's husband, Lord Mortlake. He has need of its healing powers. The griffin was taken from the Witchwood, which is my domain. It too would be useful to my lord. I know for a fact that they planned to come here to your bog lands, searching for a dragon. Have you seen these children? Do you have news of them?"

Tears stung Elanor's eyes. She had thought Wilda was their friend and ally. Tom had taken her a griffin's feather to heal her blind eyes. If anyone had told Elanor that Wilda was in league with Lord Mortlake, she would have defended her hotly. Yet here Wilda was, standing beside a smiling Lady Mortlake, betraying Elanor and her friends and their quest with every word.

Sebastian's hand pressed her arm, again bidding her to be quiet. In the dimness, he looked pale, but angry and determined. He put one finger to his lips.

"Who is this?" Lady Ravenna demanded.

"This is Wilda, the Grand Teller of Frostwick Castle, lately returned to our service," Lady Mortlake answered. "She believes these troublesome children traveled this way, seeking a dragon, of all things. Have you seen them?"

Lady Ravenna's hand clenched on her purse. She hesitated, clearly thinking how best to answer, and perhaps, Elanor figured, how to best make money out of the situation.

Jack cast a quick glance up at the minstrel's gallery, then darted forward and fell to his knees before Lady Mortlake. "Yes, my lady. I'm so glad you are here! I was trying to get word to you. Lady Elanor of Wolfhaven Castle is here! And her squire. They have come to Crowthorne Castle for help and refuge."

Lady Mortlake turned sharply and looked at Lady Crowthorne. "Is that so?"

"It is," the old lady replied, crossly. "They turned up, wanting me to send out messages. Of course I lied and promised I would. They are safe up in their rooms. If I had known you were interested in them—"

"I want them."

"Do you? Well, I'm sure we can come to some kind of arrangement. They're nothing to me. Pesky nuisances, demanding I spend good money with no guarantee of payment. I'll be glad to be rid of them. But what of the other two children your Teller spoke of? I've not seen the likes of them around here." She paused, throwing a sidelong glance at Lady Mortlake.

"Of course, I could have my Beast hunt them down for you. There's none better than he at finding those that don't wish to be found. I could send a raven to him immediately—"

Lady Mortlake sucked in a hissing breath. "Yes—"

"—for a *price*," Lady Ravenna finished with relish.

There was a long pause. Then Lady Mortlake pulled out her purse and flung it at the old woman's feet. "Bring me the children."

Lady Ravenna smiled cruelly as she turned to her guardsmen. "Send a raven to the Beast. There's hunting to be done."

10

ESCAPE FROM »——→ »—CROWTHORNE

E lanor shrank back into the curtains. They smelled
musty and old. She could hear the *tramp, tramp,*
tramp of boots as the soldiers ran up the stairs, searching for her and Sebastian.

"She's going to set this Beast on Tom and Quinn,"
she whispered urgently. "We need to get out of here.
We need to find them first."

"We must wait till all is quiet," Sebastian whispered
back. "Later, when everyone is asleep, we'll find that
sewer Jack was trying to slither through."

Elanor wrinkled her nose. "Do we have to?"

"Just joking," he said, grinning. "It'll be guarded
now, anyway. We'll find the postern gate. Lady

Ravenna seems the type to make sure she always has an escape route."

So they waited.

At first, all was noise and confusion. People shouted and ran up and down stairs and argued and laid blame. Lady Ravenna was displeased. Lady Mortlake was furious.

Elanor and Sebastian stayed crouched behind the curtain leading to the gallery.

Eventually all grew quiet. The candles were snuffed, the fire sank to ashes. The only sound was the intermittent grumble of Sebastian's stomach. "Sorry," he whispered.

The ladies' meal had been left virtually untouched on the table in the great hall and in the end it proved too tempting. Under the cover of darkness, Elanor and Sebastian sneaked down and grabbed what they could, devouring it beneath the table. It was all cold, but so delicious.

Halfway through their furtive feast, the night watch came marching into the great hall, carrying lanterns. They came and stood all around the table, stuffing food into their own mouths. Sebastian and Elanor could only sit, frozen, pheasant legs halfway to their mouths, eyes fixed on the boots before them, and the tips of the swaying swords. Finally, the watchmen finished and marched away. The light of the lanterns dwindled and Elanor and Sebastian were left once more in darkness.

"We'll head back the way they came," Sebastian whispered. "Come on."

Together they crept through the dark castle, trying to orient themselves. Once or twice they had to hide, pulses racing, as soldiers hurried past, or a lone servant scurried by, carrying a tray. It was very late, though. Nearly everyone was asleep.

Sebastian had grown up in a castle much like this. He knew castles often had a postern gate, a hidden door through which messengers could sneak if the castle was besieged. It was normally at the rear of the castle, protected by its own postern tower, well away from the gatehouses which guarded the castle's main entrance.

At last he found a small tower by itself, set at the

back of the castle. It had a narrow door of oak, banded with iron. It opened easily, its hinges well-oiled, onto a spiral staircase that led up into the tower and down into the castle walls. Elanor breathed on her ring so a faint light sprang up, enough for them to see their way. They hurried down the steep spiral, treading as lightly as possible. At the bottom, they came to a narrow stone archway, fitted with another heavy oak and iron door. Sebastian hopefully pushed at the latch. It was locked fast, with no sign of a key.

"There'll be a postern keeper," Sebastian whispered. "He'll have the keys. You stay down here, Ela, and I'll creep up and try and steal them. If I get caught, no one will know where you are."

"No, we have to stay together," she said.

Sebastian tried to argue with her, but Elanor refused to stay by herself. "Enough, Sebastian!" she finally hissed. "The Lady alone knows what will become of us if we're separated any further. Now quit arguing with me and get us out of here!"

Sebastian could not suppress the quick grin that flashed across his face. "Why, Lady Elanor," he said, as they crept back up the spiral staircase, "I didn't know proper ladies shouted at squires like that!" Elanor giggled.

"If only Mistress Mauldred could see me now!"

They came to a small room at the top of the tower. It was dimly lit by the glow of a dying fire.

There was a curious noise. Elanor had never heard anything like it. Sebastian stopped dead in his tracks. "Someone's snoring," he whispered.

He took another cautious step, but suddenly the air was split by a high-pitched yowling. A cat leapt up from under Sebastian's foot, scratched him wildly, then raced away, tail raised high. Someone snorted and snuffled and roused themselves up. "What-at-at?"

A taper was kindled at the fire and golden light flickered up. Elanor saw a fat man in a loose white smock, standing barefoot in the center of the room, eyes wide and startled.

"Uh?" he began.

Elanor saw a heavy bunch of keys hanging on a hook by the door and darted forward, seizing them. The keys jangled loudly.

"Stop!" the man cried, surging forward. Sebastian darted towards the fireplace and grabbed a poker. He waved it threateningly at the man, who turned and ran to the arrow slit. He thrust his arm through and must have seized a bell rope. A warning bell began clanging furiously.

"Fungus!" Sebastian yelled.

"Help!" the man shouted. "They're here! They're here!"

Sebastian grabbed Elanor's hand and they ran down the spiral stairs. Through the arrow slits in the curved wall, they could see lights springing up in the keep and hear the clatter of booted feet.

"Blast that cat!" Sebastian panted.

They reached the bottom of the staircase and Elanor lifted her glowing ring so Sebastian could try and find the right key. One by one, he tried the keys, but none fit.

"Hurry, hurry!" Elanor cried.

"I'm trying!" he retorted.

Elanor heard the door crash open. Sebastian thrust the keys into her hands as boots raced down the steps towards them. "I'll hold them off!" he said.

Then he sprang away from the door, racing up the steps, his poker held like a sword. The clash of metal against metal clanged in Elanor's ears.

Slowly Sebastian was beaten back down the steps. The attacking soldiers above had the advantage of height, and the clockwise twist of the stairs enabled them to hold their swords in their right hands. Sebastian was forced to use his left hand.

Desperately Elanor tried another key in the lock. It turned with a smooth click. "Sebastian!" she cried. "The gate's open."

"Go! I'll hold them off."

"No!"

"Elanor, just go!" He blocked a swipe of a sword. "Find the others! You can rescue me later. Else they'll have all of us!"

She hesitated.

"Please, Ela! Go!"

Sobbing, Elanor opened the postern gate. She looked back over her shoulder. Sebastian was fighting like a madman, keeping the soldiers from coming any closer. As she watched, he was knocked down to one knee, but he surged up again, cracking a soldier hard over the head with his poker.

"Go, Ela! Lock the door behind you and throw the keys away. Go!"

She did as he commanded, slipping through the gate, slamming it behind her and locking it fast. Then she ran as fast as she could down the steep path. When she reached the steps down to the town slumbering so far below, she flung the keys as far away as she could.

Then, hardly able to see through the blur of her tears, she bolted for the moors.

11

A PRISONER

Sebastian heard the postern gate slam behind Elanor as she fled.

Darkness descended. He struck out wildly in the dark with the poker, valiantly trying to hold off the soldiers to give Elanor enough time to make her escape. Muffled gasps told him that the poker had struck true, but his arm was tiring and a cold sweat dripped into his eyes.

Before long, Sebastian faltered and dropped to one knee. The soldiers rushed upon him and wrenched the poker from his hands. Hard hands seized him and dragged him up. He let himself go limp, pretending he had been knocked unconscious as he had seen Jack do earlier, hoping the soldiers would loosen their grip. They slammed manacles around his wrists.

As they dragged him up the stairs, Sebastian wondered what they would do to him. Despair filled him. Their brave quest was not meant to end like this, the four of them broken apart and alone. And Sebastian in chains, a prisoner.

His father would be so ashamed.

12

»»——→ THE ←——«« WHETSTONE

Quinn lay rigid with fear in the darkness.

She was trapped in a small arched enclosure that smelled of ashes. Quinn was horribly afraid it was an oven. She had only caught glimpses of it as she was flung down from the Beast's shoulder. She had seen ancient black beams, a huge arched fireplace glowing with light and the round dome of an old bread oven. Then she had been shoved in, feetfirst. A small iron door had been slammed shut, locking her in darkness.

Lie still, little maid. Sylvan's voice spoke gently in her mind. Quinn put up her hand and touched the wooden talisman. It was warm under her fingers. She felt the mouth move in a reassuring smile. *Lie still and be at peace. Let him think thee asleep.*

Quinn tried to slow her panicked breathing. She felt around her with her hands. Above was the curved shape of bricks. Below was gritty dust. The cold of the stone struck up through her thin skirt. That, at least, was a relief.

She strained her ears. She could hear a familiar scraping noise. For some reason, it terrified her.

"Sylvan, what is it?" she asked the oak medallion.

What goes around and around, but never gets anywhere? Sylvan's voice was tired and sad.

A *whetstone*. The Beast was out there, sharpening a sword.

Quinn felt as if she couldn't breathe. She wanted to bash her hands against the iron door, screaming, "Let me out! Let me out!"

Do not fret, little maid, Sylvan said. *Thou must wait.*

"Wait? For what?"

There was silence. For a wild moment, Quinn thought Sylvan was gone. She was truly alone!

What time of day is the same when written large,

forward, backward and upside down? The old voice reached her through the panic that had seized her heart.

"What?" Quinn could not believe it. Sylvan wanted to play riddle games when she was locked in an oven? With some hideous Beast out there sharpening his knife?

Think, little maid. Think.

Quinn thought. What time of day was the same when written large, forward, backward and upside down? Her thoughts were so scattered with terror that it was like trying to herd cockroaches, but as she focused she felt her heartbeat slow and her breathing steady. *In and out, in and out*, she thought. *Focus, Quinn.*

"NOON," she answered, "when it is spelled in capital letters."

Indeed, little maid. Noon is what we wait for.

Quinn nodded. She rested her head on her arms and prepared herself to wait. By noon, perhaps, Tom would have found her and rescued her.

The scraping stopped for a moment. Straining her

ears, Quinn thought she heard the rustle of a bird's feathers. Silence screamed at her from all around before she heard another rustle and the caw of a raven. A low rumbling filtered into the cold oven. Shivers skated up and down Quinn's spine. Was that *laughter*?

Yes. The Beast was laughing. Then the whetstone began spinning once more.

Scrape, scrape, scrape, hissed the sword.

Knock, knock, knock, thumped her heart.

13

INTO THE BOG

Tom ate as he flew, cramming bread into his mouth. Everything was dark; he could barely see the shape of the tors against the starlit sky. He thought he saw something small and black swooping ahead in the distance—a bat, maybe, or a bird—but the night was full of shadows and he couldn't be sure.

"You'll never find Blackmoor Bog in the dark," the goose girl had said. "And if you do, you'll only stumble into it and be lost forever."

"It's very deep," her grandmother had added. "You'll be sucked down and never seen again."

Tom wished he'd never argued with Sebastian and forced the little group to split up. As he flew over the moors, searching for any glint of light, any hint of life, he promised he would never argue with any of his friends ever again. That is, if he managed to find and free them all.

At last the darkness began to lift, light spreading along the eastern horizon. The griffin gave a piercing cry and swooped higher, circling in the rising wind. Tom nudged the griffin lower, eyes searching the bare, brown hills. The moors were empty and serene in the pale golden light, but he found the narrow road. It was easy enough to follow, a thin dark line through the bending, blowing grass. The goose girl had told him to follow it as far as it went, and then he would find the bog. And in the bog, he would find the Beast.

Tom tried to imagine what kind of hideous creature the Beast of Blackmoor Bog was. His throat closed over with fear. All he knew was that it was huge and hairy. He wondered uneasily just how big and strong this creature was. Bigger than his griffin?

Flying through the sky, Tom tried to make plans. First, he had to find Quinn and free her. The goose girl said that the executions were done when the sun was directly overhead. If Tom could free Quinn before noon, then the two of them could wait till the cartload of prisoners was brought up from the castle and then together they could rescue Sebastian and Elanor. Tom was relieved he had the strength and ferocity of the griffin to help him.

For a time, the road ran alongside the Rosemorran River. The river fell away as the land bulged into steep hills. The road began to climb the hill, winding from side to side, until it eventually led up to the top of a steep tor, crowned with crumbling gray ruins. Tom could see the silhouette of broken battlements and window arches. The tor cut sharply away on the far side of the ruins.

Tom soared high above the ruined castle and saw beyond it a valley about six miles across, protected on all sides by more steep tors, many crowned with massive granite outcrops. The floor of the valley roiled with mist, pouring up and over the granite like a waterfall in reverse. As the mist drifted apart, Tom could see down to the valley floor. Tufts of brown grasses and heathers stood up from wide stretches of black, oozing mud. Some were sheened with water; others were covered with moss that rippled strangely under the touch of the wind.

Tom flew lower and smelled the rank stink of decay. It made his stomach lurch. It was the smell of the bog-men, the skeletal creatures who'd attacked Wolfhaven Castle under the cover of a mist just like this. Since Tom and his friends had fled, they'd been hunted by the bog-men.

Tom remembered that the old witch Wilda believed the bog-men had been conjured from a bog by black magic. His whole body shivered. It was all too easy to imagine.

As the sun rose, the mist began to dissolve and Tom saw that there was an island in the center of the bog with an ancient, misshapen tree growing upon it. Long ago, it must have half fallen, for it was almost on its side, its roots like a tangle of writhing snakes, growing around and into a great flat rock that jutted out over the bog. Tom recognized the feathery leaves of a rowan tree, its berries just beginning to form.

He brought Rex down to land on the edge of the flat rock.

The griffin crouched down to rest, his tufted lion's tail curled around his eagle's talons.

The island was steep and surrounded on all sides by stretches of green-scummed quagmires. The smell of decay rose strongly from the mud, and Tom tried hard not to breathe it in. He quickly made his way along the jutting stone that was stained black with smoke and scattered with gray ashes and charred fragments of wood and peat. He walked around it and stopped, with one hand on the thick, gnarled trunk of the rowan tree.

The roots of the tree writhed into the great slab of rock as if seeking to tear it apart. Tom saw a dark crack in the rock, half hidden by a root. He bent down to look inside, but lost his footing and went skidding down to the bottom of the hill. His boots sank into the mud, but he clung to the long grasses and managed to pull his way out, and back to the rock.

The crack led to a small cave under the rock. Tom crept inside. Light slanted through the crack. He could see out through the roots and across the bog to the ruined castle. Then he crouched at the opening to the cave. He could see the bog clearly, its shores lined with the yellow flowers of asphodel and the fluffy white heads of cotton grass.

To one side of the rock was a patch of some plant Tom had never seen before. It had flowers made up of hundreds of red, pin-shaped stamens, each topped with a tiny dewdrop of moisture that glittered like diamonds. A damselfly flew down to a little bead of nectar, and, to Tom's utter shock, it became stuck there. It struggled, trying to free itself, but the red stamens suddenly furled around it, like tentacles, trapping it within a tiny cage. As quick as a gulp, the damselfly disappeared into the mouth of the plant.

The sight of the death trap flower heightened Tom's anxiety. He did not feel safe; it was as if eyes were watching him, waiting to pounce. He lurched out of the cave and clambered around the base of the stone, exploring the other side.

There, by the base of the hill, were the ancient remains of some huge creature. Grass thrust up through the eye socket of its massive skull. Seeing the outstretched shape of a wing, Tom realized it was the bones of a long-dead dragon. He crashed through the long grass, desperate to see if there were any teeth left in the huge skull. He soon realized they'd all been pried away, leaving nothing but gaping holes.

Disappointment overwhelmed him and he collapsed beside the useless skeleton, his head in his hands.

The griffin's gentle cry raised him to his feet once more.

He scrambled back up the rock and climbed onto Rex's back. "There's nothing here," he said. "Let's go."

14

»→ THE »────→
PEAT CUTTER

Tom flew back over the valley and soared over the ruined castle. All was still and quiet. The sun was just peeking over a cleft in the hill, its rays illuminating the stinking reaches of the bog, finding flashes of crimson and green and rust brown in what had seemed drear and gray.

Maybe Quinn's hiding in there, Tom thought. *It's the only place she could be. Maybe she's fallen and hurt herself. Or maybe the Beast has hidden her there . . .*

He guided Rex down and jumped lightly to the ground. "Don't go far, boy," he said, smoothing the griffin's golden feathers. Rex nudged him with his hooked beak, then spread his wings and leapt into the air once more. The blast of his passing almost knocked Tom off his feet.

Tom drew an arrow and nocked it to his bow, and then, slowly and cautiously, made his way around the edge of the bog towards the ruined castle. He stepped carefully, keeping as far away from mossy pools as he could, but still his foot slipped and he found himself thigh deep in mud. He had to drag himself out with the help of the tough roots of some heather.

The reeds were so tall and thick, he could barely see over the top. They scratched his arms and face, while midges hovered around, eager to taste his blood. Tom battled gamely on.

A merry whistling sound came to his ears. Tom stopped. It was the last thing he had expected to hear. He crept forward, bow and arrow at the ready, and peered around a clump of sedges.

A large man was digging at the edge of the bog with a heavy wooden shovel. He wore a loose shirt, rolled to the sleeves to reveal strong brown arms, and a pair of loose breeches. Rough clogs protected his bare feet. It looked as if he had never cut or combed his hair or beard, for wild and twisted black curls stood out all around his face.

As Tom watched, the bearded man paused, wiped his brow on his sleeve, then kept on digging, whistling once more.

Tom could see that he was cutting slabs of what looked like black mud away from the edge of the bog, piling them high to one side. He worked swiftly and methodically, as if he had done the task many times before. Tom hesitated, trying to decide whether to hide himself or to come out into the open and ask the man for help. He looked huge but harmless. Tom stepped forward and the grass rustled under his foot.

The bearded man turned to stare, shielding his eyes with one hand. He saw Tom and broke into a grin. "Wheesht, but you gave me a scare," he said. "I wasna expecting anyone to be around this early."

"What are you doing?" Tom asked, curiously.

"I'm cutting peat," the man answered. "Makes the best fire there is. It'll burn for hours, without needing to be fed again. Perfect for a festival fire."

"Really?" Tom came forward to look. "It just looks like lumps of mud. Does it really burn?"

"Once it's been dried," he answered. "I'll not be burning this lot today in the Harvest fire, but saving it for the next Fire Festival."

"Aren't you afraid of the Beast?" Tom said.

The peat cutter laughed, showing strong, white teeth. "There's no Beast," he answered dismissively. "That's just an old wives' tale. There's nothing to be afraid of in the bog, as long as you know the secret paths."

Tom was taken aback. The goose girl and her grandmother had been so terrified of the Beast and sure it dwelled in the bog.

"I've lived here all my life," said the peat cutter, "and I've never seen hair nor hide of any Beast."

"You live here? In the bog?"

"Not in the bog," the peat cutter answered. He jerked one thumb over his shoulder. "There, in the old castle. It's housed my family for many years."

"But . . ." Tom was puzzled. "I thought it was abandoned. I thought no one ever came here."

"Not many do," the peat cutter replied. "They come from the castle on the Fire Festival days to feed the bog with the blood of the wicked. But what do you do here? Are you wicked?"

The peat cutter's fixed gaze made Tom feel uncomfortable. "I ... I'm looking for a friend," he stammered. "A girl. I'm worried . . . worried she's lost in the bog."

The peat cutter's eyes narrowed. "A thin girl, with eyes as green as clear water and hair as wild as blackberry brambles?"

"Yes! Have you seen her?"

"She was left tied to the rowan tree," the man answered. "I cut her loose last night."

"Oh, thank you!" Tom cried. "Do you know where she is now? What's happened to her?"

"I have her safe," he answered.

"Please take me to her!" Tom said. "I have to get her away. It's not safe here. They come at noon, you know, to throw all the prisoners into the bog."

"Oh, I know," the peat cutter answered. "The bog must be fed, you know."

Tom stared at him.

The peat cutter smiled. "I can take you to her. Your friend, I mean. She's in the castle. It's not noon yet, you see."

"Quinn's in the castle? Can we go now?" Tom fidgeted from foot to foot, eager to go.

"Indeed, if you like." The peat cutter put his wooden shovel over his shoulder and began to stride back towards the castle. Tom had to almost run to keep up with him, his feet slipping in the mud.

The man led the way through a massive gateway and into the inner bailey, filled with tumbled blocks of stone. Far above, ravens flew up from their messy nests of sticks, cawing loudly. Little was left of the main keep but broken walls and arches. Many huge blocks of stone were cracked right in half and Tom wondered what could have caused such damage.

To one side was a building that seemed to have escaped much of the devastation. The man led the way there, opening the door for Tom. Inside was a long room with an enormous fireplace at one end. A low fire glowed on the hearth, scenting the air with a sweet peaty smell. Next to the fire was a row of domed bread ovens with heavy iron doors. A collection of battered pans and kettles hung from hooks above, along with bunches of dried herbs and wild garlic. A long table stretched the length of the room, its top scarred with dents and cuts. Tom recognized the room at once—it was the castle kitchen.

"She's just here," the man said and led the way towards the fireplace. "You'd best not disturb her yet. I think she's sleeping, for there's not been a peep out of her. Normally they scream and bang at the doors, trying to get out."

Tom stopped walking. He stared at the man. He tried to say something, but his mouth and tongue seemed stiff.

"What do you mean? Where is she?" He managed to say at last.

"Tom?" Quinn's voice was faint, filled with terror and relief in equal measure. "Watch out! He's the—"

Strong hands seized Tom by the shoulders. Tom fought, kicking, scratching, biting, punching. To no avail. The man simply swung Tom up and over his shoulder, opening up the door of one of the bread ovens with his free hand. Tom was shoved in, feetfirst. Then the oven door was slammed shut in his face and locked.

"Two birds caught. Lady Ravenna will be pleased," the Beast said. "Not bad for a night's hunting."

ELANOR ALONE

Elanor ran down the steep hill, trying not to slip and fall among the jagged rocks. Her lungs hurt. Every few paces, she cast a wild look back over her shoulder. She could hear hammering on the postern gate.

"Sebastian," she gasped. She saw him again in her mind's eye, standing defiantly against a mob of angry guards, fighting them off with nothing more than a poker. "Run!" he had commanded, and she had obeyed. She had to find Tom and Quinn before the Beast did. They had to get back and rescue Sebastian.

He had saved her. And she'd left him behind. Elanor could scarcely breathe with the pain of it.

Somehow she reached the bottom of the hill, her palms grazed from grasping at rocks, a stitch stabbing in her side. She gulped for air, then set off at a half run, half stumble, as light slowly revealed the vast expanse of the moors stretching on all sides. Tiny swifts were swooping around in vast flocks, their calls ringing across the pale clear sky. Elanor tripped on her skirts and fell, but was up again in a trice, hurrying on.

At last she reached the road. Again she looked behind her. Crowthorne Castle was huge and stern on its hill, all those slitted windows staring down at her. Lights blazed from the lower floors and the drawbridge was down. Knights were galloping out, dark shapes in the dawn light. She could hear the clamor of hunting dogs chasing after her.

Elanor broke into a run once more.

At last she reached the hill that concealed the valley where she and her friends had camped the previous day. Elanor labored up the slope. "Tom! Quinn! Quick!"

There was no answer. She called again.

A long, lean, gray shape raced over the crest of the

hill towards her. It reached her in a few strides, leaping up at her, knocking her to the ground. A warm, wet tongue licked her face. Elanor was caught between a scream and a laugh. "Fergus!"

The wolfhound wagged his tail so vigorously, his whole body undulated. Then another roly-poly gray shape was upon her, paws on her chest, licking her between little wuffs of delight. Elanor sat up shakily, pushing Wulfric the wolf cub away. "Down, boys. Down."

Fergus licked her again, and she pushed him off and got to her feet. "Where's Tom? Where's your master?"

Fergus whined and looked up at her with anxious brown eyes. As Elanor climbed the last stretch of the hill, he pressed so close to her legs she almost tripped over him. "Quinn?" she called. "Tom? Where are you?"

The valley below was empty. Elanor scrambled down the hill to the fireplace they had built out of rocks. The ashes within were dead and cold. Tom and Quinn's packs lay on their side, their contents spilling out into the grass. An empty pot. A wooden spoon. Quinn's shawl. The old book that Wilda of the Witchwood had given Quinn.

They would never have left their things lying in such a tumble. Something had happened to them.

"Where are they?" Elanor asked the wolfhound in a scared voice. "Where have they gone? Did the Beast find them?"

Fergus whined. Even Wulfric was quiet and subdued.

"Where are Quickthorn and Rex?" Panic edged her voice. "Quickthorn? Quickthorn!"

A whinny answered her. The unicorn stepped out from the shadow of the oak. His silvery-dun hide was the same color as the bleached brown of the blowing grasses, the faint stripes on his legs the same shape as the crisscrossed shadow of the branches. Until he had moved, the unicorn had been invisible. He tossed his head and whinnied again, pawing the ground with one huge black hoof.

Tears of relief sprang into Elanor's eyes. "I thought you were lost too!" Elanor ran to throw her arms around the unicorn's neck, burying her face in his long black mane. He smelled of turned earth and fallen leaves. Quickthorn nudged Elanor with his muzzle. His eyes were wild, the black iris rimmed with white.

"What is it? What's wrong? What has happened?" Elanor cried.

In answer, Quickthorn nudged her so hard she was almost knocked off her feet again.

Elanor was so scared she could hardly breathe. Something had gone horribly wrong. Quinn and Tom were gone, and the griffin too.

Elanor tried to steady her breathing and think about what to do. Should she gallop back to the castle and try and rescue Sebastian on her own? Or should she search for Tom and Quinn? Elanor had never had to make such a hard decision on her own before. All her life, she had been told what to do and when to do it. Ladies do not argue. Ladies do not make decisions. Ladies do what they are told.

But there was no one to tell Elanor what to do anymore. She was alone and had to act on her own. The animals gazed at her with anxious dark eyes. The unicorn pawed the ground.

Elanor pictured Crowthorne Castle and its immense thick walls, the ranks of black-and-white clad guards with sharp swords and pikes, and the cold-hearted ladies plotting within its walls. She took a deep breath, tucked Wulfric under one arm and led the unicorn to a boulder so she could scramble up onto his broad back.

"Fergus, find Tom, find Quinn," she ordered. "Find them!"

The wolfhound barked in excitement and put his nose to the ground. He ran back and forth, then found a scent trail. Elanor kicked the unicorn forward, holding the wolf cub before her. As they cantered over the hill, she looked to the castle. Dogs were racing up the road towards her, followed by running men. The sound of the dogs baying chilled her blood. They were only minutes behind her.

"Run, Quickthorn, run! Faster than you've ever run before," she urged him, kicking her heels into the unicorn's sides.

Quickthorn broke into a gallop, following the running wolfhound. Fergus had his nose to the ground, his shaggy tail streaming behind him. Elanor looked behind. The dogs and the hunters had seen her and were gesturing to the knights on their horses behind. The knights began galloping after her, the air filled with the thunder of hooves.

Elanor bent lower over the unicorn's neck. His stride lengthened.

The road led deep into the moors, over swift-running brooks and through stands of heather and gorse. The unicorn didn't slow for a moment. Elanor held the wolf cub close, gripping the unicorn's black mane with her other hand. Soon, the road steepened and Elanor saw that it led up to the ruins of a castle. The sun was now a quarter of the way up the sky. She heard a shriek and looked up, startled. A dark winged shape swooped above the castle, screeching in rage.

It was the griffin.

It was all alone in the sky. No one clung to his back.

Elanor's heart thumped hard. Tom was in trouble, she knew it. The griffin was distressed. His cries echoed around the bare slopes.

Elanor galloped across the stone bridge, then

pulled the unicorn up and slid down to the ground, dropping the wolf cub at her feet. She looked around her. The knights were galloping up the hill towards her. She had to find a way to keep them out!

An ancient portcullis swung above her head, red with rust. Elanor drew her dagger and began to saw away at the rope that held it up. She heard the pounding of the horses' hooves driving closer and closer. They were only a few strides away. The knights all had their visors down, their swords drawn. Elanor sawed her little knife back and forth, back and forth. The rope slowly frayed, but it was still as thick as her wrist and the knights were coming in fast. Tears of frustration and panic rolled down her cheeks.

"Please!" she muttered, not even sure to whom she was praying. "Please!"

With a sharp whinny, Quickthorn slashed the rope with his horn and the portcullis rattled down. The knights had to rein in their mounts hard. The horses all reared and plunged, froth blowing from their mouths. A few knights were thrown to the ground in a jangle of armor.

Elanor laughed out loud in relief.

"Got you!" she mocked. Her governess, Mistress Mauldred, would not have approved at all.

Then she turned and ran.

16

→ THE → →
TRAVELER'S STONE

Elanor raced down a long tunnel, her skirts caught up in both hands. Fergus and Wulfric ran with her, their nails clicking on the stone floor. Quickthorn was beside them, black horn gleaming faintly. From behind, Elanor heard shouting, neighing and the shriek of metal on metal. She wondered how long it would take the knights to destroy the portcullis.

At the far end of the tunnel, she hesitated. Ahead lay a valley filled with pools of slimy water and oozing black mud, broken here and there by patches of land crowded with rushes and waving grasses. The ruined castle brooded to her left, dark windows gaping.

"Quickthorn," she whispered, "a ruined castle is

no place for a unicorn. I think I need to go on alone. Will you wait for me? Find somewhere to hide and stay safe. I'll call you when I need you."

Quickthorn shook his head so his black mane flew in the wind. But Elanor was sure it wasn't safe for him in that broken castle. Quickthorn was a wild creature and safer in the wild places. She stroked his velvet muzzle and whispered, "Please, I won't be long."

At last, the unicorn slipped away into the bog, leaving Elanor with an awful hollow feeling in her chest. Behind her, the knights were pounding away at the portcullis, trying to break through. She couldn't go back. She could only go forward.

Elanor crept towards the castle, her pulse thudding in her ears. The crumbling castle seemed a dark, cruel place. Ravens swept around the broken tower in a black storm of wings, screeching defiance at the griffin. The griffin screeched back. "Rex! Shhh!" Elanor called. The griffin quieted and came down to rest on the tower height.

Eyes could be watching me from any one of those window slits, she thought to herself. But she had to go in. She had to find Tom and Quinn.

Fergus had lost the scent. His ears and tails sunk low, he cast around from side to side, trying to find a trace of his beloved master's smell. He whined and looked at Elanor.

Elanor stood still, thinking. After a long moment, she brought her hand to her mouth and breathed gently on her moonstone ring.

"Help me find my friends, Traveler's Stone," she whispered. "Oh, please, help me."

The soft silver light sprang to life in the heart of the ring. The light was different than usual. Instead of illuminating all around, the ring sent out a long, narrow beam that pointed the way forward. Elanor walked forward, her golden slippers silent on the stone.

The light led her towards the only building still standing, basking in the midmorning sunshine. Elanor noticed a garden had been planted in old tubs and broken barrels, growing herbs and vegetables. A wooden shovel leaned against the wall, its blade still wet with clods of mud. Stacks of peat were set to dry. The door stood half open.

Elanor boldly put out one hand and pushed it open a little farther. It creaked slightly. She paused, her heart thumping so hard it seemed to knock against her ribs. There was no sound. She pushed the door open a little farther and slipped inside an old kitchen.

It was empty. She looked around, wondering who lived here. The room was hazed with smoke from a peat fire which smoldered in the fireplace. It smelled sweet and heady. Hanging on one wall was a heavy hooded cloak of dark animal fur. Beside it was a heavy coil of rope and a long sword, with a handle of writhing dragons.

"Tom? Quinn?" Elanor whispered. "Are you here?"

She heard a muffled banging noise. Elanor looked around, but could see nothing unusual. The banging was somehow metallic. Fergus and Wulfric whined. Fergus ran back and forth before some bread ovens, then stood on his hind legs, sniffing at one iron door.

The banging came again.

Elanor clutched her hands together. A strong beam of light shone out from her ring, pointing towards the ovens. Elanor quickly unbarred one and swung the door open. Quinn lay inside, her skin and hair gray with ashes. She flinched away from the light. "Quinn!" Elanor cried. "Quick, quick! Let's get you out!"

She helped Quinn squirm out of the narrow cavity. She was filthy, her face white, her eyes red rimmed. She flung her arms around Elanor. "You came!" she cried. "You saved us! Quick, Tom!" Quinn unsteadily reached for the second oven.

With Elanor's help, they unbarred the oven and helped Tom out. He was as gray with ashes as Quinn, but his forget-me-not blue eyes were snapping with anger and he was not as unsteady on his feet.

He hugged Elanor, too. Then he rubbed his eyes with his sleeve, and said, "We have to get out of here! Before he gets back. We can't be caught by the Beast again."

"The Beast?" Elanor asked.

The door clicked shut behind them.

"Well, well, well, isn't today my lucky day?" A tall, bearded man loomed in front of the door. "Sent to catch two birds and here I have three in my snare."

He fixed Elanor with an intense stare. "And where did *you* come from, little bird?"

Elanor seized a poker from the hearth and swung it in front of them.

"Stay away!" she cried. "We're leaving this cursed place!"

The Beast crossed his brawny arms. "And where will you go, little bird?" Leaning forward, he rasped, "Where could you go that I could not hunt you down?"

The poker in Elanor's hand began to shake. "Hunt me?" she whispered.

Tom put a hand on Elanor's shoulder. "Where's Sebastian?" he muttered. Tears pricked at Elanor's eyes.

"He was taken. He kept fighting so that I could get away from Crowthorne. We have to go back for him."

The Beast laughed. "Too late for that, little bird. The boy has been condemned to death. They will bring him to me as they do all the doomed and damned." He nodded at the sword on the wall. "One swing, then it's into the bog he goes."

The three friends stood frozen with horror. The

Beast began to walk forward menacingly. "One, two, three, four for the bog. My lady will be pleased."

Fergus growled and launched himself past Elanor, a great streak of fury. He lunged at the Beast's throat. The man fell with a crash.

"Run!" Tom cried, snatching up Wulfric.

Quinn couldn't run. Her ankle was swollen and sore. Elanor helped her hobble across to the door, Tom supporting her on the other side.

It was hard to get past the Beast, but all his strength was being used to keep Fergus from biting him. The three children were able to escape past him and into the courtyard.

Tom whistled and Fergus let go and raced after them. Then Elanor and Quinn together slammed the heavy oak door shut, while Tom rammed the long handle of the shovel through the door handle.

"Hopefully that'll keep him for a while," Tom panted. They could hear a clatter and thumping from inside the kitchen. Then, with a muffled roar, the Beast launched himself at the door. The door shook under Tom's hand. He jerked his hand away and led the girls across the courtyard as fast as Quinn could move. Behind them, the door shuddered under another blow. Elanor cried out in terror.

"It's solid timber," Tom reassured her. "And this castle is very old. That wood is so aged, it may as well be iron."

Elanor gulped in a breath and nodded. "Now what?" she asked.

"Now," Tom replied grimly, "we wait for Sebastian. You heard the Beast. They'll bring him here today."

"Noon," Quinn gasped. "The executions are at noon."

Tom nodded. "Follow me, I know a place to hide."

SEBASTIAN AND THE WITCH

The cage was so small that Sebastian couldn't straighten his back. He had to sit hunched over, his face pressed against his knees.

Soldiers in black and white marched before and behind the procession, pikes pointing towards the sky. Ahead, Lady Ravenna and Lady Mortlake rode on fine mares, their manes and tails braided.

Sebastian ached all over with bruises. The soldiers had been rough with him, angry that he had fought them so doggedly and angry that Elanor had been able to escape. By all accounts, Lady Ravenna was not pleased.

Now he swung in a cage like a condemned criminal,

a trap to lure out his friends. Obviously, Lady Mortlake did not have as much faith in the mysterious Beast as Lady Ravenna did. She wasn't taking any chances when it came to recovering the unicorn and the other three children.

Around him, the soldiers spoke as if he was not there.

"That thief should be locked up in the cage with him. After all, it's his fault all the other prisoners escaped."

"He's with that other lady. Under her protection. I heard her say he's too useful to her to be throwing him into the bog."

"Lady Ravenna has set the Beast to find that other girl, the one that got away. He'll catch her for sure. How can a skinny lass like that get away? Impossible."

Sebastian did not like this talk of beasts and bogs at all. He scanned the horizon, looking for any signs of his friends, but the moors stretched away as far as he could see, rough and brown and bare. He felt torn. If his friends fell for Lady Mortlake's trap, they would be seized and all would be lost. But if they did not come,

Sebastian was doomed anyway. Lady Mortlake would take him with or without his friends.

They'll come, he reassured himself. *And we'll defeat this Beast and those evil women, and we'll find that dragon and get out of here.*

But no griffin came swooping down from the sky, talons raking; no unicorn galloped over the ridge. No arrows sang, no wolfhound leapt. Sebastian had never felt so alone.

He had not wanted to leave Ashbyrne Castle and go to Wolfhaven. Sebastian had wanted to stay at Ashbyrne with his family. But his father had insisted that all squires had to be fostered out to learn independence, and his mother had been busy with his little sisters. When Sebastian had begged to stay home, his father was furious. "You're thirteen now! It's time to start proving yourself a man!"

Sebastian had tried. He'd done his best to impress Lord Wolfgang with his prowess at mob-ball and jousting, wrestling and swordplay. Lord Wolfgang had not even noticed. He was so wrapped up in his grief for his dead wife he noticed nothing. Like Lord

Wolfgang's own daughter, Sebastian might as well have been invisible.

Then, when Wolfhaven Castle had been attacked and he'd been sent on this crazy, impossible quest, Sebastian had seen it as a chance to prove himself to his father and Lord Wolfgang.

It had become so much more, though. For the first time in his life, Sebastian had found friends.

And now he had lost them all, because of his own stupidity.

Sebastian found it hard to breathe with such misery in his chest.

Trudging along behind the cage were Jack Spry and Wilda, the witch of the Witchwood, leaning heavily on her ash staff. She still wore her rags, her matted gray hair hanging down her back. Sebastian stared at her furiously.

"Why did you do it?" he asked her, gripping the bars of the cage with both hands. "Why did you betray us? We gave you a griffin feather to heal your blindness. I don't understand. You helped us escape Lord Mortlake before, didn't you? What's different now?"

There was a long pause, but at last the witch said: "I was once the Grand Teller of Frostwick Castle, you see. But Lady Mortlake, she wanted no rival to her power. I was getting old . . . having trouble with the stairs . . . and losing my sight. So they cast me out, with no more care than if I'd been an old boot. I managed to find my way to the Witchwood, where I'd grown up. For more than a dozen years, I've lived there alone, scrabbling not to starve or freeze in winter."

Sebastian could imagine how hard it must have been for the old hunchbacked woman, but he refused to feel any pity. "So why are you helping them? Don't you want revenge?"

"Yes, but I want my old position back even more," she answered. "And if Lord Mortlake succeeds in his bid for the throne, I'll be the grandest Grand Teller in the land."

"So Lord Mortlake *does* want to take the throne . . . but it's impossible. King Ivor cannot be overthrown. He puts an end to all attempts of rebellion. Everyone knows that."

"But Lord Mortlake has strong magic on his side.

His wife and her sister have spent years studying the darkest lore in the land. They are both very powerful indeed. I could not stand against them. With their help, Lord Mortlake captured the unicorn and conjured an army from the bog. His lady goes today to raise another, for, I must say, you and your friends have depleted their forces considerably."

That was some comfort to Sebastian. He tried to muster courage by sneering, "Then what use are you to them, if they're so strong and powerful?"

"Well, they want the unicorn back. Its horn has the magical power of healing, which means that Lord Mortlake's army will be virtually immortal. I was able to tell them where you were heading next, so they could hunt you and the unicorn down."

Sebastian shook his head in despair.

He imagined Elanor alone, facing a battalion of armed men. He imagined Quickthorn being lassoed with ropes, his horn hacked from his noble head.

Wilda put her wrinkled face close to the bars. "Besides, I have more to offer Lord Mortlake now . . . I can bring him a dragon."

Sebastian's head snapped up. He stared into her blue eyes, bright with malice. "What? What do you mean?"

She put one gnarled finger to the brooch that pinned her ragged shawl around her shoulders. Sebastian jerked forward. It was his amber cloak pin!

"But that's mine!"

"You gave it to Lady Ravenna in return for her sending out a message on your behalf. Lady Ravenna gave it to me in return for my silver tree talisman. She's afraid of Lady Mortlake's black magic, and I convinced her that the tree talisman was protection against such dark enchantments. If she knew the truth of the cloak pin, she would never have given it to me."

"But why? What is its power?" Sebastian stared furiously at his pin.

Wilda leaned even closer. "You foolish boy. You really do not know what you gave away, do you? I knew what it was as soon as I held it in my hands."

"What? What is it?"

"This golden stone contains the trapped soul of an unborn dragon. If the stone is put in the heart of a ritual fire, at noon on any of the eight festival days, the dragon shall be reborn." The witch cackled with laughter. "Really, it is most amusing. You came to Blackmoor Bog searching for a dragon, not knowing that you carried it with you the whole way."

Sebastian could only stare at her in silence. He couldn't believe it.

"The dragon will bond with whomever breaks open the egg with fire. If you had not been so stupid, it could have been you. But you gave it away for nothing, and so now it is mine and the dragon shall be mine too." The witch caressed the smooth amber stone, then hid it away out of sight again.

"Give it back! Lady Ravenna never sent out any message for me. She lied. She *stole* that from me!"

Wilda smiled wickedly and Sebastian could only grit his teeth and clench his fists.

Wilda went on. "And you know the best thing about hatching the baby dragon? It'll give me access to a whole lot of dragon teeth. Do you know what dragon teeth are used for?"

We need one to awaken the sleeping heroes, Sebastian

thought, but did not say.

Wilda had not waited for him to answer. "If you sow dragon teeth in the bog, you will conjure an army of dead warriors. That is how Lady Mortlake has been doing it. She came here a year ago and collected all the teeth from the skeleton of the dead dragon under the rowan tree, and she has been throwing them into the bog every Fire Festival Day, summoning the dead as she needs them. One dragon tooth can call up a thousand bog-men. Lady Mortlake has only one tooth left, though. Think how glad she'll be to have a live dragon with a mouth full of teeth." The old witch cackled with laughter.

The road tilted upward and Sebastian had to cling to the bars to stop himself from being tossed around. On either side the moors stretched away, bleak and bare under a wide blue sky. The sun was almost directly overhead. Sebastian felt a crazy laugh bubbling at the back of his throat. Who would have thought it would come to this? His friends, scattered among the lonely moors. Him in a cage, to lure them into Lady Mortlake's evil grasp.

"Once I have my dragon, I'll have as many teeth as I want," the witch whispered. "Dragons grow as many as two hundred new teeth every year. If I cast them all into the bog, I'll be raising an army of two hundred thousand bog-men every year."

Sebastian pressed his hands over his ears. He did not want to hear any more. But the witch kept whispering to him.

"King Ivor cannot possibly stand against such a force. No one can! Lord Mortlake will be King and I'll be the most powerful witch in the land."

"My father will stop you! My father and his army will be marching towards us now. No one's ever defeated him. He'll have you all on the run."

She grinned widely, showing brown stumps of teeth. "You think so? You think your father is coming to rescue you? How can he be when—" she leaned in close to be sure he could hear her, "—he knows nothing about what has been happening?"

"But we sent him a message . . ." Sebastian's voice failed as he realized that they had tied their messages to the legs of birds called down by Wilda.

"Do you think I was stupid enough to actually let those messenger birds fly out? Those birds flew nowhere, you fool. The only message received was the one I sent to Lady Mortlake, telling her where you were."

"Get away from me!" Sebastian shouted.

Laughing, Wilda hobbled away.

Sebastian saw Jack Spry's horrified face and realized he had heard every word. The thief knew just how stupid Sebastian had been.

"You too!" Sebastian shouted. "Go away!"

Lady Ravenna and Lady Mortlake looked back at the commotion and Jack slipped out of sight behind the cage. Sebastian hid his face in his arm again.

Where were his friends? Did they care so little for him that they'd make no attempt to save him?

18

SKULL REVERSED

"Quickthorn!"

Elanor called the unicorn and he came trotting out from the bog, ears pricked forward. His mane and tail were tangled with burrs and his legs were thick with mud to his hocks.

Together, Tom and Elanor were able to hoist Quinn onto the unicorn's broad back, and then lead him through the swamp, following the faint and twisting path that led to the rowan tree island. Tom put the wolf cub up in front of Quinn, but Fergus had to follow close behind, his ears and tail sunk low. He did not like the bog. Several times he had slipped into the quagmire and had to be pulled free. Now it looked as if he was wearing long black boots all the way up to his belly.

Once they reached the island, Quinn slipped down to the ground, but her ankle gave way and she almost fell. She reached and grabbed a fallen branch that lay nearby. It was long enough and sturdy enough for her to lean all her weight onto it.

"There's a hidden cave under the stone," Tom said. "It's not very big. If you girls hide there, then I'll fly Rex up to the top of that tor and hide up there. When they bring Sebastian, I'll wait for a chance to swoop down and grab him. Then I'll fly away with him."

"What will we do?" Quinn demanded.

"You'll have to get away, too. In all the confusion, they might not see you escaping around the side of the island. If we can hide Quickthorn in the bog, then you can call him and gallop away."

"We have to stop Lady Mortlake raising any more bog-men too," Elanor said. "And what about the soldiers? We can't fight them all off."

"Then I'll have to distract them. If I shoot enough

arrows at them, and if Rex swoops at them enough, maybe they won't notice you."

"A lot of maybes," Quinn said.

"Any better ideas?" Tom asked, exasperated.

She shook her head.

"We just need to rescue Sebastian and get away," Tom said. "There's no dragon here; we'll have to keep searching."

"There was once a dragon," Quinn said. "I saw its bones."

"Yes, me too," Tom said. "But all the teeth are gone."

There was an unhappy silence. Elanor roused herself. "I'll try and find somewhere to hide Quick-thorn. At least his coat is almost exactly the same color as all those long gray grasses."

On the far side of the island was a bank of waving sedge grass and rushes, and Elanor was able to persuade Quickthorn to lie down in them, his head resting on one foreleg so his horn was hidden too. As she hurried back to the cave, she looked back over her shoulder. The unicorn was invisible. Elanor marve-led at how well he was able to camouflage himself wherever he was in the wild.

Tom showed the two girls the cave and told Fergus to stay with them, then pulled out his flute and called the griffin. In moments, he was soaring up to the tor on the far side of the valley and hiding behind the outcropping granite rocks at the top. They all were acutely aware of the sun creeping ever higher into the blue arc of the sky.

"Now all we can do is wait," Elanor said, sitting cross-legged on the floor of the cave, the wolf cub in her lap. In the gloom, the stench of the bog seemed overpowering. Elanor tried to breathe as shallowly as possible. Quinn stretched her swollen ankle out in front of her and examined it in the faint light from the mouth of the cave.

"Running was probably not the best thing do on this ankle," she said wryly. She looked around her. "I'll read the tell-stones. I haven't had a chance to since we left the Witchwood. Maybe they will tell us what to do."

She untied the bag of tell-stones from her belt, then, with her eyes closed, took four pebbles out of their bag and laid them at the four points of the compass. The two girls bent their heads together to examine the round white stones, all painted with simple designs.

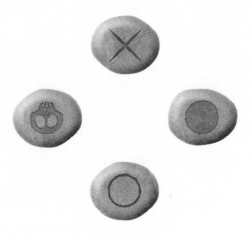

"The first is Crossroads," Quinn said. "That means a place of transition, or a dilemma."

"Well, that's true enough," said Elanor.

"The second stone is Dark Moon."

Both girls were silent. They had seen that stone before, and it was always bad news. It meant darkness, fallow times and black magic.

"Oh, but look!" Quinn cried. "The next stone

is that of the Full Moon. That means light and new growth and white magic. That's a good sign!"

"But look!" Elanor pointed with a shaking finger. "The last stone is the Skull. That means death."

For a moment Quinn was silent, but suddenly her face was suffused with color. "No! It's upside down. That's Skull Reversed. It means the cauldron of life. That's a very good sign."

"Let's hope the tell-stones speak true," Elanor replied. "For I really cannot see how we are all to come out of this mess alive."

19

»—→ NOON »—→

The road grew steeper.

Some sort of commotion was ahead. Looking up, Sebastian saw the broken castle on the heights. Ravens screeched all around it, disturbed from their nests. Knights on horseback were milling around on a stone bridge. Sebastian could see that the portcullis had been lowered. Everyone was shouting. Lady Ravenna looked furious.

Hope stirred in Sebastian's heart. He looked up at the sky. The sun was high—it was almost noon. He seized the bars of the cage and shook them again. But it was hopeless. He looked around, searching for some sign of rescue. Jack Spry was nearby, his face thin and white and anxious. Sebastian glared at him.

"Blackmoor Castle was once a great keep," the witch Wilda said. She was staring dreamily at the castle ruins. "But long ago, the dragon that guarded the blessed rowan tree was killed. The valley was cracked from side to side, and all the water of the lake was swallowed and turned to bog."

A memory stirred. Sebastian remembered hearing that story before. Quinn had read it to them out of the witch's ancient book. There had been a man who had stolen a dragon's egg from the roots of a sacred rowan tree to prove his love for a lady. The dragon had pursued him and the man had fought the dragon and killed it. He too had died though, and the lady had wept and worn the dragon's egg next to her heart for the rest of her life, in memory of him.

Sebastian's eyes flew wide. He looked to see his brooch that the witch wore at her breast.

Wilda gave a toothless grin. "Oh, yes. How I smiled to myself when Quinn read you that story. I was the only one who knew that the dragon's egg brooch was there with us, at that very moment. I would have taken it from you then, if I had dared. Lord Mortlake's attack forced me to help you flee, otherwise he would have taken the brooch, without any help from me. I couldn't let that happen."

Nearby, the knights unharnessed the cart horse from Sebastian's cage and tied it to the portcullis. They drove the horse forward until it had dragged the portcullis a few feet off the ground. Then soldiers squeezed through and together hauled on the rope, raising the gate high again. The procession marched across the bridge and through the open tunnel. Sebastian's hopes sank yet again.

As the convoy reached the castle courtyard, they heard an almighty crack. A heavy wooden door exploded outward in a shower of splinters and a tall bearded man rushed out. He looked furious, but was taken aback when he saw Lady Ravenna sitting on her black mare, scowling. He bowed at once and began to spit out some kind of story. Sebastian was too far away to hear it, but he read their expressions. It seemed someone had lowered the portcullis. Someone had locked this hairy man up. Something had gone awry with Lady Ravenna's plans.

Lady Mortlake's red mouth stretched into a sneer. "It seems your Beast is not as powerful as you imagine, my dear Lady Ravenna. You would do well to remember that."

Sebastian stared at him. *This* was the Beast?

Just as Sebastian's spirits began lifting, Lady Ravenna turned and glared at him, and at once his stomach dropped again. She shrieked a few quick orders and Sebastian's cage door was unlocked and he was dragged out.

"Take him to the rock!"

With his hands bound, and soldiers poking him with pikes, Sebastian was forced to stumble through the bog.

The tall man dressed himself in a cloak of skins, with a hood made of a bear's snarling jaws drawn over his head, then gathered up a lidded pail in one hand and a pile of planks with the other. He was immensely strong, able to carry the two dozen heavy wooden planks as if they were matchsticks. At his waist he wore a long silver sword, and Sebastian imagined seizing it and fighting his way free.

Impossible when he was manacled and chained.

Impossible when he was surrounded on all sides by enemies.

The hairy man went first, laying down a path for Lady Ravenna and Lady Mortlake. Their dogs and horses were all left back at the castle, in care of the hunters, for too much weight on the planks would make them all sink into the mud.

Sebastian found it hard to keep his balance with his hands manacled before him and the heavy chains swinging. He almost slipped several times, and found it infuriating to see how easily Jack Spry ran over the narrow planks.

The thief suddenly slipped on the muddy plank and stumbled into the witch, Wilda. She was almost knocked off her feet, but Jack helped her up apologetically.

Not so nimble, not so spry after all, Sebastian thought to himself.

They came at last to the island in the center of

the bog, marked by a misshapen rowan tree. A long flat stone jutted out from the base of the tree, hanging over the bog below. A great bonfire had been built in the center of the stone from black lumps of peat laid over armfuls of dried heather and sedges.

"It is almost noon, we must hurry," Lady Ravenna said. "Unchain the prisoner."

"I am not a criminal!" Sebastian shouted, shaking the manacles on his wrists. Sebastian felt unsteady on his feet, but he concentrated all his energy on keeping his head high. "My father will search for me!"

"But he will never find you."

"My friends will tell him what you did . . . my father will seek justice . . ."

"Friends? What friends? I see no friends."

Sebastian's eyes burned, but he kept his composure. "You may not see them, but they are here. They'll know what you've done."

"If they are indeed here, my Beast will hunt them out once more," Lady Ravenna said. She turned and clapped her hands. "Let us begin."

The Beast took off the lid of the pail. Smoke

rose from the pail, heavily scented, like a freshly plowed field. He went to the bonfire and, using a fire spade, began to ladle hot embers into the kindling.

"With the ashes of last year's fire, I kindle this year's fire," he intoned. Under the hood of snarling teeth, his eyes were strangely bright and his breath came unevenly. He began to stalk around the fire, banging the spade against the tin pail and chanting:

> ALL HAIL, THE WIND IT BLOWS.
> ALL HAIL, THE FIRE THAT GLOWS
> ALL HAIL, THE WATER THAT FLOWS
> ALL HAIL, THE EARTH IT GROWS
> ALL HAIL, THE BOG WHO KNOWS.

Everyone chanted with him, while the smoke from the fire wreathed all around them, filling the air with an orange metallic glow.

Then Lady Ravenna brought forward a bottle of mead, and ceremoniously poured a measure into a two-handled silver cup, its sides all worked with embossed patterns that looked like entwining legs and talons and wings. One by one the ladies and the Beast and Sebastian were all given the cup to drink from. The strong honey wine made Sebastian's head swim, but they made him drink the cup down. Then the rest of the mead in the bottle was poured at the root of the rowan tree.

By now, the bonfire was burning strongly and the whole island was wreathed in brassy smoke. It stung Sebastian's eyes.

"Raise your warriors, quickly now," Lady Ravenna said, looking up at the sky. "It is almost noon."

The Beast drew his heavy silver sword and stood waiting.

Lady Mortlake muttered an incantation under her breath and waved a black velvet bag through the smoke of the Harvest fire. She went around the edge of the bonfire to the very end of the jutting stone and drew something out of the bag. Leaning forward, Sebastian saw it was an old yellow tooth, about the length of his longest finger. A dragon tooth!

With that dragon tooth, a scale from a sea serpent, a feather from the griffin and a unicorn's magical horn, he and his friends could raise the heroes that slept under Wolfhaven Castle. They could fight and beat the Mortlakes and their dark magic. Sebastian had to get that tooth.

With a great heave, he broke free from the guards and began to run down the rock. Voices shouted. Lady Ravenna screamed in rage. Hands reached out to grab him. Sebastian burst through them all.

The bonfire blazed before him. The Beast loomed up through the choking smoke, great hands outstretched. The only thing Sebastian could do to avoid him was leap right over the fire.

He jumped as high as he could. Flames clawed at his heels.

He landed on the far edge of the rock.

Lady Mortlake was screeching at him to keep back, but he raced towards her. Sebastian barely registered her words as he lunged at her. She held out one hand to try and stop him, and with her other hand she flung the dragon tooth out into the bog.

Sebastian leapt after it.

His reaching hand almost caught it. The very tip

of the old bone whispered past his desperate fingers. But it was just a hairbreadth too far. The dragon tooth fell down into the bog, and Sebastian fell after it.

20

⟫⟶ THE ⟫⟶
QUICKENING TREE

Quinn crouched in the small cave under the rowan tree, one eye to a gap between the roots. It was hard to understand what was happening above her head. She could hear chanting and smell smoke. From her vantage point she could see Wilda leaning on her staff of ash wood, looking around her with bright, expectant eyes.

"We should never have taken her that griffin's feather," she muttered to Elanor, who was crouched beside her, peering through another crack in the roots.

"How were we to know?" Elanor whispered back. "We thought she was our friend."

"Sylvan warned me. He said not all witches are

wise and not all hags are honorable. I didn't listen," said Quinn bitterly.

"What does he say now?" Elanor asked.

"He said to wait till noon." Quinn leaned more heavily on her stick, her ankle paining her.

"It's almost noon now."

"There's Sebastian," said Quinn. "They're unchaining him. He looks hurt . . ."

"He saved me," Elanor said. "He stopped the soldiers so I could escape. He's a hero!"

They heard chanting and watched as a bottle of mead was shared. Quinn shrank back as they poured the remainder of the bottle on the roots of the rowan tree, only inches from the crack through which she peered.

"We have to save him." Elanor pressed both hands together in an agony of suspense. "What can we do?"

"Sylvan, dear wise Sylvan, can you not help us?" Quinn picked up the oak medallion in her hand and stared down at the wooden face, its features surrounded by fronds and leaves.

The eyes opened and looked up at her. The

wooden mouth moved. *Little maid, where art thou?*

Quinn was confused. "Why, I'm here . . . with you."

But where are we?

Quinn thought that perhaps the Oak King had been sleeping. "We are hiding under the rowan tree, Sylvan, waiting for noon, like you told us to."

What do thou know of rowan?

Quinn's confusion grew. "Rowan is meant to be good for protection. People make stars of it and hang them above their doors and windows to ward off evil."

Go on, little maid.

"It was used to make spindles too, to protect women at their work, and cradles to keep the baby safe. Oh, and walking sticks too, to keep people safe on their journeys and to bring courage and strength."

And witches' staffs.

"Oh, yes, witches' staffs as well."

Like the one in thy hand.

Quinn dropped the Oak King in her surprise. She looked at the tall staff of wood that she was leaning on. She had never thought to wonder what kind of wood it was. She could see now that it was a warm golden color, like Sebastian's dragon brooch, and gnarled and twisted like a rowan root.

"Do you mean . . . I have found my staff?"

A witch's staff comes to her when she is ready.

"But I'm not ready."

If thou were not ready, thou would not have found thy staff.

"What is he saying?" Elanor demanded.

"He says I have found my witch's staff. That means I'm ready to work magic." Quinn was dazed.

"That's good, isn't it? You can conjure magic to fight Lady Mortlake and the Beast." Elanor clapped her hands together, then paused. "Why aren't you happy?"

"I'm not ready."

If thou were not ready, thou would not have found thy staff.

"I heard him then," Elanor cried. "He says you are ready."

"I don't know how. I don't know what to do!"

"You must," Elanor said. "You know everything there is to know about trees and herbs and magic and witchcraft. You just need to think."

Quinn shook her head, but Elanor persisted. "Think, Quinn, think."

Quinn said, "Well, rowan is called 'witchwood,' sometimes, and 'quickbeam' too. Arwen says its true name is the Tree of Quickening, because it is a tree of power, causing life and magic to flower."

So thou does know, little maid. The wooden eyes closed again.

Elanor had her eyes pressed to the crack in the roots. "Look, Lady Mortlake's going to raise more bog-men! What are we going to do?"

Quinn had to stop her.

She hobbled as fast as she could to the cave entrance and pointed her rowan stick at the plants that grew at the bog's edge. "Grow!" she ordered.

And they did.

21

RAISING OF THE
BOG-MEN

Everything seemed to happen at once.

Tom jumped to his feet, watching in horror as Sebastian plummeted into the bog. The red-haired boy began to sink at once. The harder he struggled, the deeper he sank. Tom leapt onto Rex's back and swooped down over the smoke-hazed swamp.

"Bastian!" he called. "Give me your hand."

Sebastian looked up and a wide grin split his face. He managed to heave one arm out of the bog and stretched up his hand. Tom reached down and caught it. He pulled with all his strength. The griffin's mighty wings beat, sending the smoke whirling in eddies. Slowly Tom pulled Sebastian out of the sucking mud.

Sebastian reached up his other hand and caught Tom's boot, and somehow managed to scrabble up and onto the griffin's back.

As Rex wheeled and rose, the muddy surface of the bog heaved and bubbled like thick soup. Two thousand wizened hands clawed their way free, followed by the bent and twisted shapes of long-dead bog-men. Some had their heads bent at awful angles, others trailed rotting lengths of rope. All were black and gristly.

"Bog-men!" breathed Sebastian, "I'm sorry, Tom, I tried to stop the tooth from falling in the bog, but—"

"You did all you could," Tom said.

The bog-men crawled from the mud, their wizened faces turned towards the rock under the rowan tree, where Lady Mortlake stood triumphant, her white arms raised high.

But then all the plants along the shoreline began to grow rapidly, writhing and thrashing. The reeds shot up, taller than a man, while the bog asphodel bristled like an army of yellow-flagged spears. Briars whipped around the bodies of the bog-men, grabbing them and holding them down.

Lady Mortlake drew a long black knife from a fold in her skirts. She slashed it from side to side in the air, and the briars snapped and released the bog-men. But they only managed to take a step before more briars snaked out, binding them once more.

All around the island, plants were growing at an astonishing rate. Quinn and Elanor had to force their way through a thicket of reeds higher than their heads to scramble up to the island, Fergus at their heels, the wolf cub tucked under Elanor's arm.

Bog cotton exploded outward, the fluffy white seed heads now as big as burst pillows. Writhing up alongside the sedge grass was the carnivorous death-trap flower that Tom had seen eating a damselfly. In moments, it was as large as a tree, its red tentacles wriggling out like crystal-tipped snakes.

Elanor and Quinn both drew their daggers as the Beast ran towards them, swinging his great silver sword. Fergus snarled and lunged forward. The Beast sidestepped, just as Quinn brought her long staff sweeping around. It cracked against his knee, and he fell and rolled, right into the open maw of the giant death trap flower. His sword clattered to the stone. The Beast struggled to get free, but all his limbs were stuck askew. Slowly, slowly, the tentacles all bent down and closed shut, and the Beast disappeared in its glistening cocoon.

There was no time to do anything but gasp, for other things were wriggling from the bog. Giant leeches, rearing their flat heads, scenting for blood. Huge black spiders with hairy legs and gleaming eyes as big as platters. Immense hopping toads, their warts like craters. A dragonfly as big as a horse, its translucent wings whirring.

"What is it? What's happening?" Tom called down to the girls, as the griffin wheeled overhead.

Elanor had both hands pressed over her mouth. Quinn was half laughing, half crying. "I did it!" She called back, waving her staff. "I said *grow* . . . and now everything's growing!"

Lady Ravenna shouted, Wilda screamed, the soldiers grunted as they attacked, coughing in the heavy smoke from the bonfire. Rex screeched as he dived with talons outstretched, while Quickthorn attacked from the rear, deploying his sharp horn and hooves with deadly effect.

Meanwhile, the first rank of bog-men cut themselves free of the tangling plants with sharp spears and waded from the swamp, bringing with them the stench of decay. Wilda was striking left and right with her staff, turning giant leeches and spiders and frogs and toads back into their normal size. There were too many, though, jostling around her like a rising sea.

Lady Mortlake stood at the tip of the stone, her long hair whipping in the wind from the griffin's wings. Her dagger, like all witch's daggers, was made of obsidian glass. "I knew she was a witch!" Quinn gasped.

Lady Mortlake whirled and plunged the black dagger into the breast of a giant frog leaping towards her. As it crashed down, a leech reared over her. She cut off its head with a single stroke. As the bog-men struggled to be free of the tangling brambles, she pointed her glinting black dagger at the children. Her eyes were wild in her blood-splattered face. "Seize them!"

The soldiers ran to obey. Elanor and Quinn looked very small and very alone, standing back-to-back on the edge of the stone.

Tom and Sebastian together were too heavy for the griffin, so Tom brought the laboring beast down to the island. He and Sebastian jumped down and stood back-to-back with the girls, fighting desperately. Tom fired arrows as swiftly as he could, Quinn wielded her staff and Elanor stabbed and thrust with her silver dagger. Only Sebastian had no weapon. He bent and grasped the Beast's silver sword and brought it up swinging.

The plants wove themselves around the ankles of the soldiers, tripping them over, binding their limbs. Giant mosquitos hovered and darted and stung. The death trap flower seized struggling men in its red jaws and closed over them, sucking them from view.

"Get that witch girl!" Lady Mortlake screamed. "The growth magic is coming from her!"

Wilda's hand flew to her shoulder. "I'll deal with her, my lady!" But then her expression changed to one of horror. "It's gone! My dragon brooch is gone!"

"Here, Sebastian, catch!"

Sebastian glanced back over his shoulder and saw Jack Spry flinging something towards him. A gold flash. It seemed to spin over and over, in slow motion.

It was his dragon brooch.

Automatically Sebastian reached out one hand. He caught the brooch and closed his fingers tight around it. Then he lunged forward, and thrust the brooch deep into the red heart of the fire.

The bonfire exploded. Sebastian fell back in a vicious spray of sparks. There were screams as embers rained down. Sebastian sat up, cradling his burned hand. He peered into the middle of the bonfire. Something was moving.

A tiny dragon was sitting there, ears pricked. Its scales were golden red, its eyes as blue as the hissing flame. It launched itself at Sebastian, knocking him back down to the ground. Its scales were not burning hot, as Sebastian feared, but only warm. It licked Sebastian's face with a long forked tongue as blue as its eyes.

A bog-man rushed at them, spear held high. The

baby dragon turned and spat fire. The bog-man burst into flame. It turned and ran, bumping into others. The fire spread quickly. *Whoosh!* One bog-man after another fell into ash.

Tom's eyes lit up. "Fire!" he said. "They hate fire!"

He thrust an arrow into the bonfire till it began to smolder, then shot it at a bog-man. At once, it burst into flame. Jack Spry leapt forward and began to use the Beast's shovel to fling embers at the bog-men. The baby dragon spat flame at anyone who came too close. Still, it was a losing battle. The five children were surrounded, and Wilda the witch was working with all her strength to change back the giant leeches and mosquitos and toads that had been fighting for Quinn. Lady Mortlake was charging towards them, her face contorted in fury.

"What's that noise?" Quinn said, glancing around her.

Everyone fell silent and listened. The air was filled with an eerie creaking noise. It grew louder and louder.

Then Tom cried out, "Look!"

An immense winged skeleton rose up from the

bog, its bony wings flapping. It was the bones of the dead dragon.

"I must've raised that too," Quinn whispered.

The baby dragon bounced up and down on Sebastian's shoulder, shrieking with glee. The dragon skeleton bent its great bony skull in acknowledgement. Then it landed heavily, its wings knocking bog-men head over heels into the swamp.

Lady Mortlake drew herself up and raised her left hand high. The huge ring on her hand flashed with red fire. Quinn darted forward. "Oh no, you don't!" she cried. She lashed out with her staff and hit Lady Mortlake right across the knuckles. The red shimmer rising from the ring died away and Lady Mortlake screamed in pain.

"Quick!" Quinn cried. "We have to get out of here."

She scrambled up onto the bony spine of the dragon skeleton's back, and Sebastian jumped up behind her, the baby dragon twined around his upper arm. Elanor swung herself onto the unicorn's back and Quickthorn began to gallop away, cutting a path through the jumble of people and bog-men with his sharp horn. Fergus bounded close behind.

Tom was already on the griffin's back, soaring away into the sky, Wulfric held firmly before him.

Jack was left behind, his face white.

The dragon skeleton swooped around. Sebastian held down his hand. A grin lit up Jack's face as he was hauled up behind the others.

Then the dragon skeleton soared away.

22

DRAGON TEETH

The dragon skeleton flew steadily westward, towards the setting sun. Its shadow rushed over the meadows and fields below, occasionally passing over the galloping unicorn, Elanor crouched on his back, Fergus loping at her heels. The griffin soared high above.

Lower and lower the sun sank, and the dragon skeleton sank with it, wings beating slower and slower. Then the sun dropped into the sea, turning the heavy clouds to crimson and gold. The dragon dropped too, plummeting straight down. Quinn cried out in fear. As the bones dropped, they fell apart. Quinn and Sebastian and Jack tumbled down, head over heels.

Jack turned a series of deft somersaults and landed on his feet. Sebastian's baby dragon gripped the back of his jacket tightly, flapping its wings hard, slowing his descent just enough for him to land with a thump.

Quinn only had time to grasp the other end of her staff, bringing it up so it was level with the horizon. "Float!" she gasped.

Her wild descent slowed just enough for her to land and roll without much more than a few bumps and grazes. Quinn sat up and drew her staff close to her, staring at it in wonderment. She could not believe the power it carried.

It is thee who has the power, little witch, Sylvan said to her.

"I wish Arwen was here to see it," she said in a rush.

Perhaps the time will come when thou can show her, the Oak King said.

"Will it be soon?" she asked wistfully.

I cannot see so far, little witch.

Quinn got up and only then realized that they had fallen on the edge of a very high cliff. Hundreds of feet below, the sea thundered and crashed on rocks.

Another few moments, and the dragon skeleton would have fallen apart over the ocean.

"Lucky!" Sebastian said, getting up and straightening his jacket and running his hands through his wild hair.

The baby dragon had flown over to the tumble of dragon bones, and now perched on the gigantic skull, keening softly.

"Never mind, little fellow," Sebastian said.

"I think it's a girl," Quinn said. "In all the storybooks, the queen dragons are golden."

Sebastian went and picked up the little dragon, stroking her silky scales. "Never mind, little maid." The dragon snuggled into his chest.

Rex circled down so Tom could slip down to the ground and join them, and soon Elanor caught up, Quickthorn's silvery coat darkened with sweat. Fergus limped in soon after, dusty and footsore.

"We've come so far," Elanor panted, stretching out her back. "Where do you think we are?"

"Look!" Tom pointed. "Surely that's Wolfhaven Castle?"

Quinn looked across the dusk-shadowed fields and forest. A castle rose from mist, its four towers silhouetted against the colorless sky. Her breath caught. It was indeed Wolfhaven Castle. Their home. They all stood and stared at it. From out here, it looked as though nothing had changed. It was almost as though they could walk back into the castle right now, and everything would be just as it always was. Quinn would go to the Grand Teller's tree and find Arwen amongst all her books and scrolls. Tom would be back at work in the kitchen alongside his mother, surrounded by the aromas and bustle of the busy heart of the castle. Sebastian would be in the jousting yard with the other squires, with Sir Kevyn bellowing at them. And Elanor would be back in her lonely room, being scolded by Mistress Mauldred.

Quinn sighed. Even with Sir Kevyn's bellowing and Mistress Mauldred's scolding, it would have been good to have been back home. Glancing at her friends, she could see her longing reflected on their faces as well.

"Look!" whispered Elanor. A light shone out from the window of the highest tower. Quinn wondered who it was, sitting in the warm glow of lamplight in Wolfhaven Castle, when the castle's lord and all his people were captured and enslaved. Was it Lord Mortlake? What other wicked acts was he plotting by that golden light? A lump rose in her throat.

"So, what do we do now?" Jack said.

"We go on with our quest," Sebastian said. "You . . . well, I guess you go on sneaking and thieving, like you always do."

His voice was not unkind, but Jack hung his head.

The little maid is lonely, Sylvan said to Quinn.

She jerked upright. "Little maid?"

Jack looked at her sideways.

"You're a girl?" Quinn said.

Jack had flushed red.

"A *girl?*" Sebastian repeated.

"How did you know?" Jack asked Quinn. "No one has guessed for such a long time."

Everyone gazed at her in astonishment.

"But why pretend to be a boy?" Quinn asked.

Jack jerked one shoulder. "When my parents died, I was left all alone. It seemed safer to be a boy."

"Have you no family left at all?" Elanor asked.

Jack shook her head. "Don't need any. I'm fine on my own," she answered belligerently, but Quinn thought her eyes told a different story.

"What is your real name?" Elanor asked.

The girl shrugged. "I was named Isibail."

Sebastian laughed. "I don't think I could ever call you that. It's far too girly!"

She looked away, her color rising. "My parents called me Isi. But I've been Jack for so long, Jack is my name now."

"So where will you go, Jack, what will you do?" Tom asked.

Jack shrugged.

"You could do me a great favor," Sebastian said after a moment. "Would you take a message for me to my father? He does not know what has happened at Wolfhaven Castle. You could ask him to raise an army and march to their aid. He should let King Ivor know too. Would you do that for me?"

Jack nodded, her eyes shining. "I'll be sure to tell your father how brave you were," she said.

Sebastian turned as red as a beet. "I couldn't stop Lady Mortlake raising another thousand bog-warriors," he said. But then he grinned. "I did get us a baby dragon, though!" He tried to stroke the little creature on the head and the dragon turned and snapped at him. "And she's got plenty of teeth!"